The Wedding at Shepherds Pass

Alex Mitchell

Published by Alex Mitchell, 2024.

THE WEDDING AT SHEPHERDS PASS

First edition. November 20, 2024.

Copyright © 2024 Alex Mitchell.

ISBN: 979-8891980303

Written by Alex Mitchell.

Also by Alex Mitchell

I dedicate this book to Ashley and Nathan. May your journey into the loving institution of Marriage bring you all the joy life has to offer.

Chapter One: Ambush

B ased on a recent event that ended the lives of several U.S. marshals transporting prisoners from the Shepherds Pass Courthouse back to secured federal facilities, new methods were put into place to safeguard all involved in the process.

Prisoners were loaded on the courthouse grounds under the watchful eye of the U.S. Marshals. The Shepherds Pass Police supported the marshals and the Shepherds Pass Sheriff Deputies. The bus carrying the prisoners back to the prison where they were being kept was escorted by two police cars, one in front and one in the back of the bus.

The new escort process for prisoners seemed flawless. However, like most things that appear flawless, one has to know where to look to find or start the flaws.

During this transport, an unexpected police car flashed its lights and pulled out in front of the trailing police car for the detail, causing the follow-up car to stop.

"What do you suppose that was all about, Bossman?" Clinton Easterman, the driver of the busload of male prisoners, asked his supervisor, Vincent Stapleton. Vincent Stapleton was a grey-haired veteran of transport who had seen almost every situation that could arise during transport. He had personally been involved in foiling three different prisoner liberations in his 28-year career.

"Not a clue. I am going to call the house and see if there is a change of plan no one told us about." Stapleton stated in a commanding tone.

Stapleton attempted to contact the prison, but the radios would not work; there was only white noise. Stapleton took out his cell phone, which would not allow a call.

There were three guards on the bus, Clinton Easterman, Stephen Ryerson, and Vincent Stapleton, with the prisoners secured and locked behind a steel fence in the bus. This secured arrangement should have been sufficient. But Stapleton was starting to worry. About a half mile further, the lead police car crossed the railroad tracks, and the gate to stop traffic immediately fell. This put the lead escort on one side of the track and the busload of prisoners on the other side of the track. A train with a single car pulled out and stopped. Slowly, the door to the freight car opened, and there were several men and an unusually looking gun. The gun was a M134 minigun.

"Oh, shit, back up," Ryerson yelled.

While the bus passengers were observing gunmen in masks, a bulldozer pulled in behind the bus. The bulldozer grabbed the back of the bus and lifted the rear slightly. There was no way the bus would get traction to drive.

Two of the figures from the train climbed down and walked toward the door to the bus.

"We would like a moment with the guard in charge." The first voice of the two was clearly a woman as she tapped on the door window.

"LOOK, BOSS, YOU ARE less than a year from retirement. There aint no reason for you to die on the side of this road. Let me take your place." Ryerson whispered to Stapleton.

"No way, kid. This is why I get the extra twenty bucks a week in my paycheck—just for times like this." Stapleton stated, then opened the door to the bus. To the amazement of the prisoners and guards, Stapleton showed no fear.

The masked man and woman motioned Stapleton closer to begin their conversation.

"Have you ever seen one of those up close?" The masked man pointed at the M134.

"No. And I can say it gives you a real shitty feeling being on the business end of it." Stapleton answered.

"It can be set to fire 2000 or 6000 rounds per minute." The female bandit explained.

"So, what do I have to do not to let that happen." Stapleton was starting to sweat, giving away his false bravado.

"If you do exactly what we tell you, you can walk away from this. You see, I will let you in on a little secret. I have instructions that I am not to harm a single guard. But if one guard challenges us, all the guards must die," the male masked man stated.

"Then I guess you want us to give up our guns?" Stapleton guessed.

"Negative. Keep your guns. And always keep the prisoners under control. Your first instruction is to get everyone off the bus. Line the prisoners up facing us. You have three minutes to comply."

Stapleton tried not to let his confusion show. In the required time, the prisoners lined up and faced forward.

"I guess you pigs don't like being prisoners yourselves." One of the prisoners sneered.

"Shut up," Ryerson commanded.

The woman in the mask walked down the group, selected three prisoners, and ordered them to stand off to the side. A heavyset man in a mask stepped from the train, carrying a hand-help machine gun.

"Forgive me for stating the obvious, but this seemed like a lot to do to free three scumbags," Stapleton stated.

The woman walked close to Stapleton and whispered in his ear. "Kiss Jena for me." Stapleton's eyes went wide; Jena was the name of his new grandchild. "Who said anything about freeing." The masked woman smiled and waved her hand. A volley of machine gun fire annihilated the three that had been separated from the group.

One of the masked men placed something under the bus.

"Final instructions, Mr. Stapleton." Stapleton knew he had made the right choice; they knew who he was, and to try and deceive them may have had dire consequences. "There is now a bomb under the bus. You will get back on the bus, and when the timer I give you rings, the bomb is disarmed. If you try to move the bus or open the doors, it will explode."

"You will find the train car about four miles down the track without evidence. You will find we have returned the bulldozer to the worksite where we collected it. You will also find both your police escort cars with the police in the trunks." The female bandit explained.

The male bandit handed a small digital time to Stapleton, and Stapleton commanded his prisoners to reenter the bus.

"That was the weirdest thing I have ever heard of." Easterman confided to Stapleton as they waited for the clock to count down. Even the prisoners held their breaths as time oozed by.

Chapter Two: A Friend of a Freind

"Do you know what you are wearing to the wedding?" Lavon asked.

"Nothing," Abby answered.

"Another desperate attempt to stand out, Abby? When will you ever learn."

"Look, I never said I was going to your wedding, Detective Tyler." Abby corrected.

Lavon Tyler and Abby Blackwell are detectives for the Shepherd Pass Police Department. Lavon Tyler came to Shepherds Pass about six months prior.

The two sat at a table in Salvatore's Pizza Restaurant. Lavon Tyler is a powerfully built guy who boxed golden gloves and played Florida State Seminole football before enlisting in the army. After joining the military, he was a detective for the Mississippi State Bureau of Investigation. Tyler had left Mississippi over embarrassment associated with the breakup of him as his fiancée at that time. He has settled in Shepherds Pass and was now engaged to Lynn Dodd-Masterson, a local judge.

Abby Blackwell is a Shepherds Pass detective with a history of alcohol problems. Abby had dark curly hair the teased the front of her face. Through the grace of God and the help of the people of A.A., she was clean and sober for about six months. Many of the people Abby and Lavon had to encounter in their work did not like Abby due to her past. With Lavon, she seemed, however, to function well even if they taunted each other.

"If you don't show up, many people will be disappointed," Lavon explained.

The two were seated at a table, waiting for Nya. Nya is a friend of Lavon and married to Wendell, a police officer who was the first person to make friends with Lavon the day he showed up for his new assignment in Shepherds Pass.

"Name one."

"Me," Lavon answered.

"Try again."

"Momma. She is in town and says she cannot wait to meet you." Lavon answered.

"You are putting pressure on me, Detective Tyler. Somehow, that doesn't seem to fit with your rules of fair play."

"And I know you well enough to know that if you keep calling me by my real name and don't make crazy insults, you are really upset with me."

Just as Lavon was making his point, Nya showed up. Nya wore a nurse's maturity smock that boasted the full glory of her condition. Nya rushed up, took Lavon's hand, and placed it on her stomach.

"It won't be long now." Nya smiled, ignoring Abby for the moment. Abby and Wendell, Nya's husband, had been involved in disagreements in the past. Lavon had brokered a truce between Wendell and Abby and with Webber, one of Wendell's closest friends. Nya was unsure if it was her place to respect the truce, but she knew she did not like Abby, and it showed.

"Nya, if you have a crime to report need, I remind you that you sleep, among other things, right next to one every night." Abby made her presence known.

"The need is not mine. Only the introduction." Nya's snapped at Abby.

"What introduction?" Lavon asked.

Nya waved her hand, and a young black girl seated at another table came over and sat down.

"This is business I leave to you. Be careful where it takes you." And with this, Nya walked away, leaving the poorly dressed young lady with Lavon and Abby.

The young black girl had a clear complexion and looked like she washed and scrubbed regularly. The homeless look the girl gave off was a disguise, but why?

"And who might you be, young lady?" Abby asked.

"It doesn't matter. I think I was followed. Take this, and my mission is completed." The young woman shoved a wad of paper into Lavon's hand. She then started to pan the room. There was something she saw that was not apparent to Lavon and Abby. But whatever the young woman saw was sufficient to cause her to bolt from the table and run from the restaurant.

"Did that make any sense to you?" Lavon asked Abby after the young woman was gone.

"Maybe she is with the local theater group. I got to go. My babysitter is on overtime." Abby referred to her English Bulldog puppy as if it were a child.

Lavon began walking Abby to her car. He remembered their conversation before the drama of the evening.

"Look, Abby. I don't know what I am to you, but you are very important to me, so at the very least, we can talk about whatever is bothering you."

Abby stopped and shallowed as if choking down a load of pride to make the following comment. "Alright, but remember you refused to leave it alone. The problem is that I am jealous of Lynn for having you. I know it is stupid because you are the kind of guy who is one hundred percent monogamous, and I am not a monogamous person, at least not that I know of. I could ruin your life. But the other thing is that you met Lynn six months ago when you wandered into town with a broken heart. To me, it sounds suspiciously like a rebound. I don't want you to wake up six months from now looking over at Lynn, wondering what the hell did I do. If you love her and she loves you, I don't know what the big rush is."

This was the biggest block of true inner feelings Abby had shared with Lavon in quite some time. Before Lavon could respond, there was a scream coming from the alley behind the Pizza Restaurant. "Help some call the police."

"This is going to have to wait," Lavon stated.

"Yeah, they are playing our song."

WHEN LAVON AND ABBY entered the alley, there was a large woman who had obviously screamed. There was a wino who stood staring down at a pint of broken wine that lye on the ground, shattered and reeking. And there was the crumpled mangled body of a young black girl mangled and distorted. She was the same girl Lavon and Abby had met less than ten minutes ago. Lavon put his hand on his head and began walking in circles.

"Oh, no, you don't, country boy. No way you shut down that big brain on me now; we got a killer to catch." Abby shrieked at Lavon.

"He made me drop my wine." The wino cried out. "That giant the killed that little girl. Made me drop my wine. You don't know how important that is to me."

Abby researched into her purse and retrieved some bills and handed them to the wino. "Actually, I do. Now stay here for questions, and you can get another one."

"Bless you, lady." The wino praised.

"What is this all about?" Lavon asked the air.

"I just hope you kept whatever she gave you," Abby stated.

"I did. It is a list of names. I think you have to call your sitter. Looks like we have a long night ahead of us."

"DID YOU TWO MOVE IN, or are you running from the law?" Don Nash, the detectives' lieutenant, asked.

Don Nash was a recently promoted Lieutenant who had worked as a detective supervisor for Lavon and Abby. When Nash arrived at the police station, he saw Lavon and Abby earnestly at work.

"We are the law. We caught a murder last night must have happened feet away from us, and we had talked with the victim right before the incident," Lavon explained.

Nash stated, eyeing the paperwork the team had collected. "You, tracking a real desperado?"

"No doubt. There are ten names. From the list, the girl gave us right before getting her neck snapped. The youngest on the list is seventy years old." Abby commented.

"I respect a strong work ethic just as much as the next guy, but why put so much effort into a case that probably is just random mugging?" Nash asked.

"Well, remember, my partner is getting married this weekend. The last time he left, he kept checking in with me. That might fly when she was your girlfriend, but when she puts that ring on your finger, there is no way she is going to put up with you breaking from the backstroke to call another woman," Abby joked.

"There is the bitter little Abby I have come to know and love," Lavon commented.

"Don't look at me for a tiebreaker because I agree with Abby on this one. Tie up everything you need before sailing to the tropical island."

"YOU TWO ARE REQUESTED to appear in room 109 of the court building, pronto." Nash reappeared at Lavon and Abby's desks.

"Any Idea why?" Lavon asked.

"None."

THE NEW SHEPHERDS PASS court building had the handed-down regal appearance of justice through the years. There were paintings and sculptures depicting man's connection to the arts and culture as they related to fair play throughout time. However, there was still the smell of rubber molding and carpet glue. Even after almost a year, a new building trying to palm itself off as an old classic structure could not entirely escape physics.

Lavon and Abby seated themselves on the visitor's side of a mammoth desk that was littered with files, folders, and papers. A thin man in an old suit stood staring out to the window into the courtyard. A second man in his mid-thirties who looked like he had tailor issues or perhaps he had grown a size and a half since breakfast.

"My name is Malcolm Duckworth; I am with the Department of Justice. Thank you for agreeing to see us today."

The man at the window did not turn around; instead, he continued to stare out the window.

"I know those look like Canadian Geese, but they are not. They are Missouri Geese. They came here. They liked it so much we granted them political asylum." Abby stated to the man not facing the room.

Lavon tapped Abby's arm in an attempt to prevent her from causing problems.

"Detective Tyler, are you related to Andrew Tyler?" Duckworth asked.

"Yes."

"What can you tell me about him?"

"He is my older brother Norbert's son and one hell of a little league pitcher," Lavon responded.

"Could we take this a little more seriously? We are all busy people." Duckworth asked.

Lavon and Abby mirrored a mutual confused stare.

"Do you remember these three men?" Duckworth asked as he reached into a folder and lay three pictures on the desk facing Lavon and Abby.

"You arrested them for carrying loaded firearms inside the bus terminal." The man facing the window reminded.

"They later confessed to shooting your brother. Out of guilt and remorse, no doubt." The man from the window stated.

"Sir, if you came here to accuse me of something, at least have the dignity to face me," Lavon stated in a harsh tone.

"Raintree. Federal prosecutor. And son, if I wanted to accuse you of something I would not need the D.O.J. to lead the meeting. For the time being, think of me as a casual observer."

"They are all three dead as of yesterday," Duckworth revealed.

"Wow. How?" Abby asked.

"A small group of armed, well-organized people pulled their transport bus over and machinegunned them on the side of the road. No guards were injured, and no prisoners escaped."

"Looks like you guys have your hands full. Unfortunately, so do we. I get married this weekend, and I have a murder case of my own to work on."

"Judge Lynn Dodd-Masterson, soon to be Lynn Tyler." Duckworth rummaged through a different folder.

"I am warning you, don't go there." Abby pleaded. "It is hard as hell pulling him off people after they make the mistake of insulting his lady love. And besides, I just got this jacket. The last time someone said something bad about the judge, I got the pockets ripped off my jacket trying to keep him from strangling the guy. And that guy was a cop."

"Well, it would appear that the criminals that were executed were operating on Dolan Dodd territory. A future relative of yours." Raintree added.

"Detectives, I am here because the U.S. Marshals office thinks you two withhold information for your own benefit, even when it may conflict with the interest of the federal government," Duckworth said.

"Those jackasses were led on a merry romp through the woods while people here were dying on our watch in Shepherds Pass. I guess they have to report it in a way that makes them look less like a bunch of clowns. They fell for a diversion, and we lost people." Abby complained.

"This meeting is over," Lavon stated and stood up.

"Son, I don't think you are dirty. But one day, someone from that family will come to you with the information they know you need and make a devil's deal with you. Be prepared."

"IS THIS THE DESK OF Detective Lavon Tyler?" A slender woman in her early thirties stood in front of Abby. Abby had been reading reports connected to the names of the list she and Lavon had received. The woman approaching Abby wore a finely tailored suit and expensive shoes. She had a Southern accent.

"He stepped away for a moment. I am Detective Blackwell. Can I help?"

"No. It is a personal matter. My name is Lindsey Tyler."

"Well, I was expecting a Tyler invasion. I might say you dress well. Better than your brother."

"How do you know my brother?"

"Who is your friend, Abby?" Lavon asked, walking up.

"They must have bit off more of your ass this morning than I thought if you don't recognize your sister," Abby concluded.

"Ma'am, my name is Detective Lavon Tyler. Is there something I can help you with?"

"Wait, she is not your sister. Why does she sound just like you?"

Abby's comment caused Lindsey to give Abby a harsh stare. "I in no way sound like him."

"Don't be ridiculous, Abby. She is from South Carolina, I would guess. They don't sound anything like us."

"Got it in one," Lindsey informed Lavon.

"Oh God, I got to get my ears adjusted. They will probably have me drop them off and pick them back up later."

"Is it a good idea for her to be carrying a gun.?" Lindsey asked.

"No, not at all, but we like to live dangerously." Lavon joked.

"I wanted to ask what your sister, the F.B.I. agent, has planned for my brother?"

"This is sounding better and better?" Abby stated.

"I did not know I had a sister who is an F.B.I. agent."

"Anita Tyler."

"I have a sister named Anita, who is in the army. Overseas last time I heard."

"She checked into the Drake Motel with Eric this morning," Lindsey informed. "Maybe you guys should put out a family newsletter." With this snippy comment, Lindsey was off.

Lavon began putting on his jacket.

"Where do you think you are going," Abby asked.

"The Drake."

"Bad idea. Why don't I go to the Drake, and you go to the autopsy? You do dead bodies better than me, and if your sister is doing something naughty with this Eric fellow, I can either tell her to clean up her act or, if this is a different Anita Tyler, I can give her some pointers."

"Remember that poor girl, who probably only has the same name as my sister, and she and her boyfriend are enjoying some quality time. Try not to ruin it," Lavon suggested.

THE LAB CONNECTED TO the police autopsy was never designed to be a joyful place. Today, however, it was even more somber than usual. Lavon searched for Aaron Flack, the young technician who had frequently helped him.

"Where is Aaron? Did you guys finally give him a day off?" Lavon asked Burt, one of the technicians.

Burt was in his mid-twenties, thin and pale, with a perfectly manicured beard and mustache. He had large globe-like eyes and wore eye makeup.

"That's right, you are new around here. You don't have as many people telling you things as most people around here."

"Let me in, Burt. What's wrong?"

"That dead girl you sent in here last night is Aaron's little sister. As per procedure, Aaron is not allowed in the lab for a week. Chain of evidence concerns."

"I have got to go see him."

ABBY SAW SOMEONE SHE knew as she walked across the Drake Hotel parking lot. "Noreen Tyler!" Abby screamed. Noreen Tyler is one of Lavon's sisters. She and Abby had met when Lovester, Lavon's younger brother, had been shot by someone who thought Lovester was Lavon.

"Well, if it isn't the woman that keeps my blockhead brother from tripping over his own two feet," Noreen responded. "Are you ready for the wedding?"

"Where are you headed?" Abby tried to ignore the question.

"Anita is in room 14B. She said to meet her there; she has a surprise for me."

"I love Tyler surprises." Abby chuckled.

"HEY, LITTLE SIS." ANITA threw open the door and hugged Noreen.

"This is Abby Blackwell. I told you about her."

"Well, I have heard some horrible things about you. You must be cool," Anita said, hugging Abby.

"Right back at you," Abby muttered.

"Wait here," Anita stated, running out the door and banging on the next room door. Anita grabbed the young man, who poked his head out and pulled him into the room with the girls.

"Noreen, this is Eric, your escort for the wedding. Eric, this is my sister Noreen."

Eric and Noreen stared at each other. There was a commonness of concern but an underlying interest.

"Look, whoever you are. I don't do blind dates. I am sorry if my sister is so concerned that the guy I was seeing died and felt she had to take care of me."

"It's alright. She didn't tell me any of that. She said we had similar interests, and a dinner surrounded by your relatives might be a good way to meet. I assure you I am not a part of a conspiracy. Congratulations on your recent graduation."

"Would be a safe way to meet someone." Abby filled in.

"That's alright. I don't think Kim has a date, and she is at least taller than you are." Anita taunted.

"So, if he is my date, who is your date?" Noreen asked.

"Andrew Tyler," Anita answered.

At this point, Abby took out her pen and notepad. "Sorry, guys. I know there is going to be a test later. I just need to make some notes. Now, is this the same Andrew Tyler who pitches Little League for the Mississippi Wildcats?"

"Of course not. That is my nephew. This Andrew Tyler is with the Department of Justice. We met by accident, and Eric helped me contact him. He agreed to come here for the wedding."

"Does that make him Lindsey Tyler's brother?" Abby asked.

"Who the hell is that?" Anita asked.

"Is this a private party, or can anyone join?" A strong woman with a bodybuilder's frame entered, pushing the partially open door. The woman was with a teenage girl.

"Colossus?" Abby guessed.

"This is Jody Diane Tyler, my sister," Noreen answered. "Jody, this is Abby Blackwell."

"So, you are the smart mouth idiot that is supposed to watch my brothers back?"

"Be nice, lady. There are children in the room." Abby instructed.

"She can't hear me. She's deaf. So why don't I drag your sorry ass outside and teach you some manners."

"Stop that." Noreen jumped between Jody and Abby. "You know what momma says about us girls tussling among ourselves."

Jody put her arm around Noreen. "That is why people keep punching you in the face little bit. You just keep stepping up no matter the challenge."

"For my notes, who is this?" Abby pointed at Sabrina.

"This is my friend and my partner's daughter. Her name is Sabrina."

"One last question for my report. They were asking about an F.B.I. agent named Anita Tyler. Any clues to who that is."

Anita reached into a purse and pulled out her badge. "That would be me. Anita Tyler F.B.I."

A shocked wave overtook the group. "Right there, that's what I want," Abby exclaimed as she captured the shock with her cell phone camera. "This is going to be priceless."

Chapter Three: The interviews

Lavon and Abby sat on the sofa in front of Arron Flack. The Flack home was surprisingly average for the image Arron portrayed in the police lab. Arron was a small man of 5 foot 4 with a small body frame for a man. Arron was openly gay and generally outspoken. Today, however, a different version of Arron rang through. Arron sat crushed by the death of his little sister, Fiona. He was all cried out.

"I want the both of you to know I don't blame you in the least."

There was limited comfort for Lavon or Abby as Arron struggled to focus his eyes.

"Tell us about your sister?" Abby asked. Abby and Arron had had a rocky relationship in the past. Abby had been prone to homophobic slurs, and anger rages toward Arron, but this was all on hold. The competent investigator in Abby was starting to rise to the surface.

"She was always my protector when we were growing up. My father could not accept the fact that I was gay. And my mother never stood up for me. He was not physically violent, but he harassed and humiliated me in a way no parent should ever be allowed to treat their own child."

"Arron, she was dressed like a homeless person. Any idea why?" Lavon asked.

"Those damn T.V. shows she was so obsessed with."

"What T.V. shows?"

"True crime and cold case T.V. shows. Someone commits a crime, but no one has ever caught on." Arron had now accessed his reserve tears as he thought about his sister's mistake.

"You think she stumbled across something that is going on, and someone killed her to keep it quiet?" Abby guessed.

"Arron, I need you to look at this list of names and tell me if there is anyone here you know." Lavon requested.

It took only a glance, and Aaron shot up from his lethargy. He ran to his bedroom and returned with a framed pitcher of his sister and an older woman. Both women in the photo were wearing running clothing. "That is Charlotte Garcia. She was a friend of my sister. That was taken at one of the 5k races. I don't remember where."

"Galaxy Plus Gym sponsored it, that's their logo. I am a member." Abby responded.

"Lavon, I know what you can do. I have seen you in action. I know you are getting married in less than a week. I know what you can do in a short time. I am begging you, please help me." Arron requested, then turned to Abby. "I know we don't really care much for each other, but please keep Lavon safe."

"OFFICER WEBBER, IT'S nice of you to join us." Duckworth sat behind the desk in the court office wearing another of his ill-fitting suits. Raintree sat at a separate table, scribbling something.

"Well, Sir, if you are with the Department of Justice, you are most likely a lawyer, so does that mean I need legal representation?" Webber asked. Officer Webber is Detective Tyler's friend and Sargent Wendell Bishop's close friend.

"Well, let's hope it doesn't come to that. But at any point you feel uncomfortable, please feel free to request we stop and reconsider where we are. Are you and Detective Tyler close?" Duckworth folded his hand in front of himself.

"What do you mean by close?" Webber asked.

"Well, let's say, have you ever been out with him after work?" Duckworth clarified.

"Yes, we have sat down to a beer a couple of times."

"Twice?"

"No, maybe more than that. Maybe four or five times."

"Considering he is new in town, that seems like a lot. But you two are not romantically involved, is that correct?"

"Okay, so that just set off my discomfort alarm. I am married, and he is getting married at the end of the week."

"I am sorry if I offended you. My question is to determine the best way to phrase my important questions. Believe me, your answer would have little bearing on my questions, only how I phrased them. You see, my wish is to observe and show respect for what you referred to as your comfort level."

"Then no, Lavon and I have no romantic involvement."

"Lavon, don't you mean Detective Tyler?" Raintree chimed from the side desk.

Webber did not respond because she did not want to, but she was distracted by Duckworth laying down pictures of the men who had been killed after the marshal's bus had been attacked.

"What can you tell me about your assisted arrest of these men?' Duckworth asked.

"I heard some guy got taken off a bus and capped, but I had no idea who they were." Candidly, Webber confessed.

"Are you and Detective Blackwell good friends?" Raintree asked.

"No."

"Have you taken the Detectives or Sergeants exam?" Raintree asked.

"No. Why?"

"Because maybe you should. When I read this report on where everyone was and what they did at the arrest, it seemed more to me that you were not assisting her. She was assisting you."

"MAN, YOU COULD HAVE knocked me down with a feather when I found out Abby was a cop. And a freaking detective at that." Butch, an overly muscular man in day-glow spandex, stood behind the Galaxy Plus gym counter, addressing Lavon. Abby has suggested to Lavon that they split up and she interview the home of Charlotte Garcia to save time. Lavon suspected there was more than that to Abby's suggestion, but he went along with it all the same.

"You know Detective Blackwell personally?" Lavon asked.

"I haven't seen her since those assholes killed her sister Doris in the parking lot."

"Yes, that was bad." Lavon now knew precisely why Abby was avoiding the gym.

"I went out with Doris a couple of times," Butch confessed.

"You don't say."

"She was all about the sex. I kind of wanted a relationship, but when I mentioned that she went cold. Funny how different women can be."

"Do you know Charlotte Garcia?"

"New past tense. She died like eight months or so back."

"What can you tell me about her?" Lavon asked.

"Real shame she had that accident. The old girl was in better shape than many of my younger regulars. She hung out with a group of old people who seemed to be staying in shape to stick it to the grandkids." Butch chuckled.

Lavon took out his list. "Are any of them on this list?"

"Hilarious, pal. That is the entire over-the-hill gang."

WHILE ABBY WAITED FOR Alisa to finish waiting on a customer, it was easy for Abby to see why this donut shop was so popular with the police and firefighters of Shepherds Pass. The place was spotless. All the people working looked like they had been driven through the human equivalent of a car wash. The worker had all been scrubbed within an inch of their lives, as had Alisia. There were no bazar piercings, strange hair colors, or even visible tattoos.

"Young lady, I am going to ask you some questions. Nothing is meant by the questions, so try not to be offended. The more you answer clearly and directly, the better I stand at doing my job. Do not guess or make anything up if you do not know the answer. Are we clear?" Abby instructed.

Alisa was a small girl of Hispanic descent in her mid-twenties. Her large, dark eyes seemed to call you to stare at them.

"My report tells me your grandmother, Charlotte Garcia, died from a fall downstairs last year. Is this correct?"

"Si. I mean, yes, ma'am."

"This was an accident."

"No, ma'am. It was not an accident. She was murdered. I told the cops. My grandmother was in better shape than they are. No way she fell."

"And what did they say? The cops, I mean?"

"They started reading me some statistics about the number of people over an age that fall. But that was not my grandmother. She was in great shape. She ran in races to collect money for charity."

"Did your grandmother come into any sudden income?" Abby asked.

"No, she was poor but had what she needed to live on. We had to pass the hat to cover some of the expenses when she died."

"Did she have insurance policies?"

"One that I know of to cover burial expenses. And as I said, it wasn't quite enough."

"Do you know this girl?" Abby showed the running picture to Alisa.

"Yes, she is Grandma's friend.

"How did they meet? Who do they know in common?"

"I don't know, but they have been friends for a while. But I told all this to Gunderson."

"Who?" Abby shouted, not knowing it was her own voice that made her shake.

"Detective Gunderson and his pal. They questioned me, and I only remember the man Gunderson because how he looked at me made me want to wash."

"CONGRATULATIONS ON making Sargent. And congratulations on the upcoming new addition to your family." Duckworth stated as Sargent Wendell Bishop sat in the same chair Webber had only a couple of hours ago.

"No offense, sir, but could we get to business? Whatever this business is. I have work to do."

"Yes, I understand you are the best man at a wedding this weekend."

"You have gone through a lot of trouble, so on the other hand, take your time."

"This won't take long Sargent. How is it that you happen to be available on your day off to back up Detectives Tyler and Blackwell at the bus station."

"Sir, a big part of what I do as a Police Officer is to protect and serve the public. The other part of what I do is to back up and assist other officers who need my help. I do not discriminate against friends over officers I do not know or like. If they need my help, I will be there.

When a detective says he needs help with three men that might be armed, I have no answers because I ask no questions."

Duckworth looked as though the interview was not going well and dismissed Wendell.

Chapter Four: The light of Life

"Lynn, baby, try not to fidget so much." Rebecca Tyler requested. Rebecca Tyler was in the process of measuring Lynn for a dress. Rebecca Tyler had always felt that being the mother of fourteen Tyler children was God's greatest blessing. Rebecca Tyler loved children and became a schoolteacher to help educate and mold the young. Samuel Rowen Tyler and Rebecca were married young. The push to increase the size of their family had always come from Rebecca. Rebecca was now a thin-framed woman with silver hair that she often wore in a bun. Rebecca wore heavy-looking glasses that were no doubt for their functionality instead of being worn for fashion.

Rebecca was now a grandmother, and all the joy being a parent brought her was magnified by being a grandmother to her many grandchildren. As mother and grandmother, there had been bumps and mishaps along the way, but love had always found a way to rule supreme.

Now, Rebecca knew her mission was to impart any wisdom and assistance she could to Lynn. The first child can not only be frightening but also confusing. Rebecca and Lynn met when Lavon brought Lynn to Lamont, Mississippi, to participate in the charity athletic games. Lavon had broken off his engagement with Carrie. Rebecca had known Carrie when she was in school. Rebecca did not disagree with Lavon's decision to marry Carrie. Still, Rebecca was aware that Carrie had the tendency to commit to a dare by friends no matter how foolish and no matter how lasting the results were. Rebecca had wished Carrie would outgrow this before marriage. Rebecca also knew her seven sons well enough not to ask the details as to why certain things transpired as they did because the boys have always been honest with her, even when it hurt. And Rebecca saw no need to extend the pain Lavon would be experiencing. That is why when Lynn contacted Rebecca to tell her that Lavon had been injured attempting to arrest a murderer, she felt relief that Lavon had someone close to him who was concerned about his wellbeing. Rebecca's mission had never been to take over her children's lives. However, as a schoolteacher, she knew people did their best when supported properly.

Now, in front of her was Lynn. Rebecca knew Lynn had been widowed from an earlier marriage and had never had children. Love for her son seemed to gush when Lavon's name was mentioned.

"You know you don't have to do this; I can afford to buy a dress," Lynn reminded her future mother-in-law. Lynn, Rebecca, and Kim were in the master bedroom of the stone semi-mansion that Lynn owned.

Rebecca put Lynn's arms down by her side to take a measure, and Lynn quickly raised them back.

"Kim, do me a favor and find your father. He is going to the police station here, and I need you to help keep him out of trouble," Rebecca instructed.

"Will do, momma." Kim saluted and was off, leaving Lynn and Rebecca alone. Kim Tyler was nineteen and had a boyish frame. Her breasts and curves, if on order, had as yet to arrive. Kim displayed energy and enthusiasm that were mysteriously rooted in the core of her being.

"I don't understand. I have a wedding dress."

"Yes, and you will wear that for your wedding here in Shepherds Pass. But our family has a homecoming celebration for newly married couples where you are officially welcome into the family."

"Oh God, Mrs. Tyler. I am so taken by how well you all treat me; it sometimes gets a little confusing. My own mother doesn't treat me as well. And you are making me a dress."

"My dear child, let us clear up a couple of things. Sit," Rebecca Tyler instructed and patted the side of the bed. First, dressmaking is an almost lost art in this country. But before it dies completely, all my girls will appear in church wearing a dress I made for them."

"I am not really one of your girls." Lynn tried to highlight the discrepancies.

"Yes, you are, which brings us to our second point. Now, you don't have to call me momma if you feel like that would insult your natural mother. But you will stop calling me Mrs. Tyler. Mother Tyler will be just fine."

"Yes, Mother Tyler." Lynn smiled.

"Good. Now, let us address the elephant in the room, so to speak."

"I have no idea what you are talking about." Lynn blushes slightly.

"Well, for starters, would you like for me to build a little extra room in the front of your dress because you may be showing by the time you make it to the church reception?"

Lynn looked around the room as if someone might hear them talking. "How did you know?"

"Baby, I am a mother and a schoolteacher. I am a grandmother and an aunt to quite a few. You don't think I can look into the eyes of one of my own and know she is carrying the light of life around with her."

Lynn hugged Rebecca and could not speak for a while.

"My only question is that if you are carrying my son's baby, why you are keeping it a secret from him? I suppose if he knew, he would have been doing cartwheels on the front lawn when we drove up."

"Because I proposed to him," Lynn answered.

"And you don't want him to think it was some trick or ultimatum."

"What I want more than anything is to build a relationship based on trust. I feel strange being the first one in our relationship to be the one asking." Lynn paused and then continued, but she needed someone to express what she was going through. "After I proposed, I got up from one knee, and I was dizzy The next day, during a court session, I had to bolt to go throw up in a trash can."

"The first one is often like that. Your body is getting you ready to have children, and there is no way of knowing if you plan on having just the one or fourteen like yours truly." Rebecca informed Lynn. "And if my son has any reservations, tell him to come see me. Remember the night of the closing of the charity events? I told you, girls, I was short of grandchildren compared to some of the other grandmas. I distinctly remember telling you girls to go home and put your back into it."

Rebecca sat with Lynn, having the mother-daughter talk that Lynn had never had. The fact that Lynn was a well-educated judge meant little when it came to what was happening inside her.

"ABBY, THIS GUY SAYS he is here to see you." Barney, a middle-aged, heavy-set Detective, walked up carrying boxes like he was winded from the effort. Barney laid the boxes on Abby's desk, and a shorter gentleman in an expensive suit stepped from behind Barney. Abby looked at that man; it took only seconds to recognize who he was. Abby pushed Barney out of the way and threw herself into an ardent hug around the visitor. "I know who you are."

"Who am I?"

"You are the chief. My knucklehead partner's father." Abby stepped back and then hugged Sam Tyler again. 'I'm sorry the last couple of days have been kind of shitty it is good to see someone who won't make my day worse. I guess it is sinking in that your son is going to leave me here solo for a while."

"No need to apologize. At my age, an old man gets up in the morning hoping for an unsolicited hug from a beautiful woman to whom he is in no way related."

Sam Tyler tapped on Abby's desk for Barney to put the boxes down, then gave him a lollipop. "That will be all my good man."

Samuel Rowen Tyler was a retired police chief and had become a writer. S. Rowen Tyler, as he was known in writing circles, served in Mississippi as a small-town police chief after leaving the army and had a noteworthy career. He had not only reduced the crime rate but maintained a balanced budget and was noted in a newspaper article as the great man. The great man was now a joking nickname for friends and relatives. Sam Tyler's first books did not sell well. After it became known, however, that he was writing S Rowen, Tyler became known as the go-to guy to write biographies for F.B.I., C.I.A., and other agents that wanted a book on their careers published. This boom in popularity led to Sam Tyler writing stories about legendary cases and events. Sam would change in the name of those involved in his books. Rebecca, his wife, being a retired schoolteacher, began editing and correcting his work, and the couple had a project that sealed their connectedness in their retirement years. Sam Rowen Tyler had also been known to assist some of the agents in solving crimes as payment for their stories. Sam chose to keep his activities in the active case as clandestine as possible, especially from Rebecca; to her, those were her golden years, and he owed them to her entirely.

Barney looked at Abby with a look of amazement on his face.

"He is messing with you, Barney. He is a retire police chief, he probably wrote the book on how to pick on detectives."

"Your son is busy pulling records for a case we are working on."

"Good. My daughter Kim insisted on coming, and I distracted her by letting one of the cadets show her the gun room. Poor bastard has no idea she knows more about guns than he ever will. So, we had time to talk."

"Great, you are even more devious than I imagined," Abby confirmed.

"Kim is a good girl, but at her age, she should be somewhere in the back seat of a beat-up car, letting some poor bastard know where the boundaries are. Instead, she chooses to spend her time waiting on me and her mother's hand and foot."

Abby laughed and placed her hand over her face. "I think it is cute that she is following you around."

"My dear, she has started to hover over me and her mother like a pack of cute little buzzards hovering over a nursing home."

Abby began to inspect the boxes.

"Open that one. It is from me."

"You don't have to buy me presents. I am not the one getting married." Abby stated, ripping open the package.

"Oh shit, I can't take this." It was a Glock 19 gen 5.

"Sure, you can. None of my kids go without the proper protection."

"I have a service weapon?"

"Good, now you have two. My son was regaling me with a story about how you fought off two bad guys, one with a machine gun and the other with a shotgun, and you had a modified starter pistol."

"It was not a started pistol. It was a .38 Smith and Wesson."

"And they make great guns now, but that thing you had was for back before the bad guys were not so well armed."

"Well, we were alone in my bedroom. I have a home-court advantage when I have guys in the dark at my place."

"And if you plan to shock me with some dirty cop talk, you will have to try harder. I wrote the book on that too."

Abby fiddled with the gun as she wrestled with how to ask Sam Tyler what was really on her mind.

"Did he tell you about my problem?" Sheepishly, Abby asked.

"Dear girl, I was a cop long before you or my son was born. My children have grown to know that many things I have encountered in my life will help them decide their path going forward. So yes, my dear Abigail, he did tell me about your drinking issues. I have known hundreds of cops with drug and alcohol addiction problems. It takes a lot of courage to deal with it, and I salute you."

"Oh, Chief why are there not more guys like you."

"Most guys are the product of what has happened along to way to make them what they end up. Good and bad experiences affect the outcome."

"Don't tell your son, but I like him a lot," Abby confessed.

"Good because he loves you," Sam informed.

A shocked look came over Abby that was clearly blood rushing from her head.

"No, he loves Lynn."

"Yes, he loves Lynn. She is his romantic love. But you and my son have entered into what I call the covenant of the blood. You have killed for him, and he had killed for you. You are now bonded uniquely. I have seen countless detective teams undergoing many marriage changes but keeping the same partner in the field. I have talked to many a cop that would take back an old partner that he or she trusts but would never think twice about taking back an ex-wife or husband."

"SO, WHAT DID YOU THINK of my father?" Lavon asked Abby. They walked through the park surrounding the man-made lake in Shepherds Pass. A manmade lake had been built to add to the aesthetic beauty of the area. Several restaurants face the lake and offer alfresco dining. Two higher-end motels also faced the lake, providing a view for their quests. Lavon and Abby were looking for a street artist who went by the name Visionary. When examining the list of ten names Lavon and Abby had given by Fiona, it was clear that three people with check marks were dead. All three deaths were listed as accidental. All three were handled by Detective Zeb Gunderson and Detective O'Leary, who worked as a team. Lavon knew he was now walking a fine line, but it had to be navigated. He was investigating the murder, but maybe he was also investigating police negligence on the part of two detectives or, at worst, police corruption. Lavon and Abby had met Gunderson at Zeb's Magic Touch. The retired Detective Gunderson now owned a beauty salon that catered to older women. Gunderson had admitted to removing police files and replacing them with blank paper before his retirement because those files incriminated the mayor of Shepherds Pass in a rape.

"I like him. I can see how he can inspire the team to do its best.'

"Now my mom is jealous. She wants to meet you. I guess it will break her heart to hear you don't plan to come to the wedding."

Abby made a face, but before she could respond, the two spotted a young girl sitting against a tree with a sketch pad. She appeared to be drawing a pair of old men who were on a bench playing chess.

"Are you the Visionary?" Abby asked as she and Lavon approached.

"There is no, The, in it. That would be like referring to Prince as the Prince. I am Visionary. And you two look like cops."

"Thank you," Lavon commented.

Visionary was in her mid-twenties and wore a multicolored bandana. She wore a tee shirt and old jeans suitable for sitting on the grass.

"You are standing in my light," Visionary informed Lavon.

"Sorry." Lavon excused himself and stood off to one side.

"God, I love old people. They move so slow I could pound out a statue of them with a hammer and chisel in a big ass rock and still have time for coffee breaks."

"We want to ask you a question about an accident," Abby notices Visionary is now staring at her.

"Can I touch your hair?"

"No."

"Then my memory is getting a little fuzzy for whatever you two want."

"Look, Rembrandt, I don't do girls." Abby snapped.

"Well, I do, and I do boys two, but you are not my type. I am an artist. What I want to feel is the texture."

"Look, young lady." Lavon began.

"Okay, touch my hair, but if you do something strange, I swear I will pulverize you." Abby leaned forward to allow Visionary to touch her hair. The touch took only a few seconds.

"Was it good for you?" Visionary joked.

Lavon chuckled, which did not lighten the look on Abby's face.

"An old man. Jose Pacheco was run over in an accidental hit-and-run last year; what can you tell me about the accident?" Lavon asked.

"Nothing," Visionary answered.

"Turn your back. I am going to bitch slap this fool." Abby asked Lavon.

"Don't get hormonal on me. I can't tell you anything about an accident because there was no accident. The fat guy ran over the little Mexican guy on purpose."

"How do you know that?" Lavon asked.

"The fat guy sat in his car and waited with the motor running until the little guy got into the middle of the street. Then he raced for him. The little guy did a spin move suitable for the N.F.L. to get out of the way, but fatty adjusted and sent the little man sailing."

"The Detectives interviewed you at the time. Did you tell them this?" Abby asked.

"Yeah. They did not seem interested. The red-headed one squeezed my ass. So, I think I know where his mind was, but he seemed more into pain. I enjoy the pleasure side of things." Visionary reached into her backpack, pulled out a sketch pad, and tore out a couple of pictures. "Here is the fat guy. Sorry, he never got out of the car, so the picture is not that clear. And here is the two cop's girl watching."

"Damn," Abby stated as she looked at the likenesses.

"THERE YOU TWO ARE. I guess you joined that Ivy fellow in trying to besmirch the names of good old-fashioned cops." Detective O'Leary ranted as Lavon and Abby returned to the police station squad room. O'Leary hated Lavon. Lavon had been involved in a charity boxing match that had permanently crippled a former detective that was a close friend. Lucas, the detective that was cripple, had been an abusive lover of Abby in the past. O'Leary stood over Abby and Lavon's desk, holding some of the files they had been collecting for their investigation.

"What is your problem now?" Lavon stated in an angry tone.

"Look, you ape. The last time you guys wrestled, you two ripped the pocket off one of my favorite sports jackets," Abby said.

"You sleazy, tart as always, you are at the root of the problem." O'Leary accused.

Lavon took a step toward O'Leary.

"Slow down. What the hell is going on?" Don Nash, the Lieutenant, yelled.

"This clown is going over things on our desk," Abby stated.

"These two heroes are pulling old cases that I have already closed. Probably looking for punctuation or spelling errors to report to the internal investigations clowns on the fourth floor." O'Leary was now in a sweat.

"We got time for cold cases. I thought you were closing things out so you could dance with your new wife on a beach somewhere. And why does this place look like we are opening a bakery?" Nash asked.

"The case we are working on is the homicide of one of our technician sister. That happened a couple of days ago. She had a list of names, and we were checking the names from the list. A couple of his cases showed up." Lavon explained.

"I don't see the harm in these two pulling information to get a lead on their case. Do you?" Nash asked O'Leary.

O'Leary angrily walked off. Abby snatched the files from O'Leary's hands as he pouted.

"Now, the bake sale?" Nash asked Abby.

"My partner's father dropped off the baking. Someone likes me."

Nash started to walk away, then stopped and turned back to Abby and Lavon. "Why do I feel like you two are hiding something from me?"

"Because we are. But don't worry, we will bring you in at the right time." Lavon answered.

"Gee, I can't wait."

"THAT'S ODD," ABBY MUMBLED to herself as she sat reviewing her notes from the day before.

"I will see you one odd and raise you one weird," Lavon said.

"Okay, me first. The Garcia girl said that they had to pass the hat to plant grandma in the ground. Still, I show two insurance companies inquiring about the death cert listed here."

"My turn." Lavon scooted his seat over to show Abby the picture he was examining. "What is wrong with this picture?"

It took only a moment for Abby to see what was causing Lavon great concern. "Where is the angle of the body?" Abby asked. "Please tell me the medics first on the scene moved stuff around."

"The victim's cane is at the top of the stairs near the door. Where she would hand placed it when she was unlocking her apartment door. The body outline is on the lowest level landing three landings down." Lavon surmised.

"She would have had to fall down the stairs, dust herself off then throw herself down to the second level. The get up and throw herself to the lower level," Abby stated.

"Or someone would have had to pick her up when she reached her apartment door and flipped her over the railing." Lavon guessed.

"Damn." Abby exclaimed and looked at Lavon knowing he was reaching the same conclusion she was. The was not incompetence. This was a poor job at a cover up.

"Have you been able to find out why my brother is coming here for your wedding, and you don't know him?" Lindsey Tyler had appeared unnoticed and causing Lavon and Abby to be startled.

"I can answer this one. But isn't your brother old enough to date?" Abby asked scrambling for her notes from the meeting with the Tyler girls.

Abby and Lavon waited for Lindsey's answer, but none was forthcoming.

"There was a mix-up at some big to do in New York, and his sister's name tag got switched with your brother's. She had her geek friend track your brother down and asked him to dance the couples dance with her since she did not have a date." Abby scrambled through the note she had taken when meeting the Tyler girls.

"What about this, Eric, Casanova?" Lavon asked.

"I met him. He is no Casanova, and he is Noreen's dance partner for the wedding. He is a friend of your sister Anita's."

Lavon sat back and smiled. "She is answering your questions, but you never answered hers."

"Well, my family is wealthy; my mother is a senator and all. I have to be sure people are who they say they are. And you said your sister is not an F.B.I. agent."

"She is not," Lavon stated.

"Ah, but she has got you on this one. Your sister is in the army but was put on loan to the F.B.I. She is scheduled for the F.B.I. academy right after you jump the broom."

A startled look overtook Lavon, and Abby captured the look for posterity with her cell phone. "She went on assignment with some Clarkson fellow."

"Waldron Clarkson?" Lavon asked.

"Sounds about right," Abby confirmed.

"My father set this up, and the reason it is hush-hush is not that it is national security; it is because my mother does not like Waldron Clarkson." Lavon assessed.

"Then I apologize to you, Detective Tyler, for jumping to conclusions and to you for any of the spiteful things I said to you, Detective Blackwell."

"DO YOU TWO COMEDIANS know how big this problem is?" Don Nash asked. Lavon and Abby had joined Nash in his office and closed the door. They had begun outlining what they had discovered so far.

"Yeah, but look at the bright side," Abby suggested.

"What Bright side? I got an amateur sleuth that finds wholes in our detective squad and gets her neck snapped doing our jobs. I got four dead bodies there that were most likely miscategorized, and I got you leaving on a honeymoon in a few days. When the news gets out, they Shepherds Pass detectives have stacked the deck on cases the line for retrials will stretch around the corner."

"I don't see the bright side either, Don, but that is what people usually say at a time like this." Abby teased.

"I would say cancel the wedding if I did not see a judge from the richest family in town get down on her knees to ask you to marry her. She is probably the last person I want to make an enemy for life."

"Well, the bright side could be that all this happened before you took over. So, it will look like you are cleaning the house," Lavon suggested.

"The only problem with that is that your friend Crawford had this job before me, and she has been promoted. If she feels I am upstaging her, she could come down on me like a ton of bricks."

"You are right. It is lonely at the top." Abby assessed.

"Go back to work, Tyler, and wrap up as much of this as you can before you leave. If you need help find whoever you need. Please take your smart mothed partner with you."

WHEN SHE AND LAVON returned from Don Nash's office, "How can we help you, sir?" Abby asked the casually dressed man seated in the guest chairs.

"I wanted to talk to the both of you."

"Well, why don't we start with who you are and why they let you wander free in this building," Lavon asked.

"Sorry." The man reached into his pocket and retrieved a badge from the U.S. Marshal's office. "I am Vincent Stapleton. My friends call me Vince. I wanted a moment of your time."

"Have some cake, Vince." Abby offered, and he accepted.

"You two are not exactly what I would have expected." Stapleton assessed.

"Why don't you tell us why you are here," Lavon asked.

"Well, I was the lead guard on that bus that was stopped on the roadway by that train the other day." Stapleton began.

"Oh, Vince, baby, that is not our problem." Abby's head dropped forward, and her long, dark, curly hair covered her face.

"Look, I aint wearing a wire. I came here to thank you."

"I don't mean to look a gift horse in the mouth, but what exactly are you thanking us for?" Lavon asked.

"Well, the other day, the guys that stopped us." Stapleton stopped and looked around to be sure no one could hear him. "They said they had instructions not to injury any guard unless we insisted. They knew

I was the lead guard. They knew my new granddaughter's name. I didn't even know I would be taking that bus until right before it was assigned to me."

"I am sure I don't want to know, but do you have any idea why they did not want to harm you," Lavon asked.

"Well, the ones that did the talking was a man and a woman. They seemed almost to finish each other's sentences."

"You mean like a husband and wife?" Abby asked.

"No, he means like police detectives that work together on a regular basis." Lavon introjected.

"Excuse me, sir, but when you were outside, did you see them building a gallows?" Abby asked.

"Look, I aint trying to set you too up for nothing. If someone shot my little brother, I might run the thought of handling it on my own. Not to say that I would, but you too got our respect no matter what the bosses are trying to put you through."

Many of the recent events started to make sense to Lavon and Abby.

LAVON HAD BEGUN TO be haunted by Abby's observation. How could someone with two life insurance policies have a family need to pass the hat to put her in the ground? Lavon and Abby contacted Alisa and had her give permission for the life insurance agent she knew of to speak with Lavon and Abby.

Lavon and Abby sat in Jesus Sanchez's office, waiting their turn to be seen. Sanchez had a small, storefront practice, but it was bustling with people who needed bi-lingual assistance understanding the insurance process. Sanchez was a man in his thirties who looked like he should be in the movies. He was clean-shaven, with thick black hair and a strong facial structure that looked like it had been handed down from generation to generation.

"Sorry to keep you waiting. Some of my clients have nowhere else to go for advice on documents written in legalese. I cannot understand that if the average educational reading level in this country is eight grade or so why are so many forms document and instructions written as if they written for nuclear physicist."

"You got my vote, Mr. Sanchez. What can you tell us about the policy for Charlotte Garcia?" Lavon asked.

"Well, it was small and inadequate, for starters."

"Come again?" Abby asked.

"Sure, let me explain. Year ago, when the Garcias bought their policies, they were more than enough to cover cost at that time. But we have only one way to safeguard against inflation and that is to increase the coverage over time. She did not."

"But you offered." Lavon checked.

"Look around you. I love my people. I love children, and I am a family man. Of course, I offered. But what happens is two things: that many from other countries start sending money back to their old country so much that it is to the detriment of their own existence here. Second, many have a conversion problem and consider what things cost back home. So, they think the little they are insured for is more than adequate when it is not."

"Do me a favor and take a look at this list. Let me know if there are any names you recognize any of the names. You do not have to give me any information on their accounts. If I need that, I will get a court order." Lavon requested.

"No, I don't think so, but our names are not as distinct as you choose yours to be. And we often use two last names, so the name on your list may not be exactly how it appears in a legal document." Sanchez eyed the list.

"Do you hold the policy on a lot of retired people?" Abby asked as she saw an elderly couple entering the small storefront office.

"You mean semiretired."

"Her granddaughter said she was retired."

"I guess that is one way to look at it. After years in the plant, they retire and get a small pension. They get social security, and the company hires them back as what they call consultants, and they work a few days a week to pick up some extra spending money. It is happening all over this country, and not just to immigrants."

AFTER THE INTERVIEW with the insurance agent, Lavon and Abby felt they better understood what was happening. Still, the information had piled on them like an avalanche, and they both needed time to consider what they had heard. Lavon decided to go for a beer before going home. Abby decided to return to the office, rescue some of her sweets, and take them home. When Abby arrived at her desk, a thin young blond girl was sitting in the guest chair writing something on a notepad. Abby was searching her tired brain for the appropriate smart-mouth remark, and the girl bounded from the chair when she saw Abby and threw her arm around her.

"Abby, I am so glad to meet you finally."

"Who are you, or should I know?"

"You are just as funny as I thought you would be. A real pistol."

"And my answer is in there somewhere, is it?"

"I am Kim Tyler."

"Jesus, now I know what it was like for that blockhead partner of mine landing in town and not knowing which Dodd was from which family."

"Papa is a writer, but I am going to be an even better writer than him."

"Well, I wish you all the luck."

"Do you have any allergies?" Kim asked.

"No, why are you shedding?"

Kim started laughing, took out a notepad, and began scribbling. Abby also took her notepad and started making notes.

"I help Momma with the baking, but I just don't want to give you anything that might cause you to swell up, especially this close to the wedding."

"Slow down, cheery person. I have no plan to go to the wedding."

"Well, that will break Bobby Joe's heart."

"Well, I am sure he will get over it." Then, Abby's face looked confused. Abby started shaking the notepad like something might fall out, but nothing did. Okay, you got me who or what the heck is a Bobby Joe ."

"Well, since you ask so nicely. He is your date for the wedding, and you have to dance the couples dance with him."

"Look here, my sunny little friend. I have been around twice as long as you, and I am not about to fall into this trap."

"And what type of trap are we discussing?" Kim asked.

"My partner is handsome, and I met Lester, not the sharpest knife in the drawer but a really good-looking young guy. How many extremely good-looking guys are allowed in one family? This Bobby Joe is probably a troll."

Kim sat smiling for a moment, then pulled out her cell phone. "This is a picture of the boys I took for last year's promotional poster for the volleyball game at the church fundraiser."

Kim showed Abby a picture of Tyler's son. All the men were in shorts without shirts and holding volleyballs.

"That one is Bobby Joe."

"Oh God and I can get some of this?" Abby exclaimed, then looked at Kim. "Sorry, I didn't mean to say that out loud."

"Oh, Abby, you are going to be a great person to write about."

"Alight, my pretty little con woman, what is the catch? Is he married? Gay a mass murderer, not that the mass murder thing would disqualify him."

"He is not married. He is the battalion commander for the Lamont Fire Department rescue team, which handles highway and emergency rescue. He was dating a girl a couple of years ago, and she left him, breaking his heart. Momma feels really bad for him she says he is scorched. He spends most of his time caring for this team and looking after Jody, my impetuous older sister."

"Why did the girl leave him?"

"For another guy."

"Who?"

"I don't know. It is not something he likes to talk about."

"No, really, who would leave this guy."

"Since you called me a con woman, I want to lay my cards on the table. Bobby Joe is on his way here. He was told by my father that he was dancing with you. If he gets here and you are not attending the wedding, he must dance with me. Now I love all my knucklehead brothers, but I think he deserves to dance at his brother's wedding with a pretty girl like you and remember that not remember dancing with his little sister."

LAVON SAT ALONE, THOUGH surrounded by revelers. He sat in Patrick's bar. Patrick's bar is one of the favorite bars for police, firemen, nurses, and anyone who is subject to work late nights or early mornings. Patrick's has a small grill that is open at all times. The sound of an overhyped pop singer mangling a country classic played, and it seemed that the guests to Patrick's were not only talking loudly to be heard but also to drown out the music selection.

Nya sat down in front of Lavon, who had not even noticed her arrival. Nya took Lavon's hand and turned his palm upward. Lavon took a big drink of his beer with the other hand.

"Might not be the best time for a reading, Nya."

"I don't have to read your palm, your feet, or the bumps on your head to know what is going on with you, country boy."

"Please enlighten me."

"You want to know if I blame you for Fiona's death."

"Do you know I was right there, and if I had taken it more seriously, she might still be alive."

Nya smiled and looked into Lavon's eyes. "I see you said you and not we. But Abby was there, too. And last time I checked, she had no qualms about vaporizing people she thought were a threat."

"It was my responsibility."

"That is why you and my husband like each other so much. You two are so much alike."

"That's a good thing, right?"

"Listen to me, Lavon Tyler. Everyone can do the right thing and the end result still be bad. Fiona was tracking someone or something that must have found out, and it started tracking her. She kept whatever she was collecting to herself too long and died as the result. She watches those TV shows where everything comes out in the end. Well this is real life and not everything always comes out alright in the end. She would still be alive if she told someone what was happening sooner."

"Do you know what that means?"

"Tell me smart boy."

"It means the best we can do is finish what she started and get to the bottom of it."

Nya stood and kissed Lavon on the forehead. "Go home and give your wife a sloppy kiss. She will need your support more than ever over the months to come." With this, Nya was gone.

Lavon sat thinking about Nya's parting words, but they seemed to make no sense as usual.

"Is this a private party, or can I join?" Officer Webber approached Lavon from behind. Lavon wondered why she may have been waiting for Nya to leave before approaching his table, but he was sure he would know soon.

"Sit, buddy."

Webber sat and stared at Lavon for a moment.

"If you are waiting for me to guess what you want to talk about, you are out of luck. See, I just had a talk with Nya, and that usually scrambles my brain for a while thereafter."

"Me too, God bless her physic soul." Webber giggled.

"Do you believe in that stuff?"

"Truthfully, I was the biggest skeptic on the planet until I met Nya. Now she has me wondering. I mean, she knows things she should not. She can sometimes tell you to look out for things. If I think about it too much, I get shivers."

"So why did you wait for Nya to leave before coming to talk to me?"

"What is that physic shit rubbing off."

"I am a cop, too, remember."

"Fair enough. Some guys wanted to talk to some of us about you and Blackwell. One guy said some things that made it sound like we were having an affair, but it's okay."

"Chubby guy in an ill-fitting suit?"

"That's the guy. Him and some old guy that doesn't talk much."

"Don't let it rattle you. It's called beating the bushes. They are doing that because they have nothing on the murders." Lavon explained. "They are probably hoping we look into it and give them a starting point."

Webber finally smiles. "You learned that stuff from your father, didn't you?"

"Yes, and I want you to meet him. He is in town for the wedding. So now tell me the other part."

"Alright, smart ass. I want to have a child."

"Can't help there." Lavon lay back and took a big drink, finishing off this beer.

"Just listen. My wife has better insurance, and she wants to carry the baby. I want Wendell to donate the sperm."

"Now we have reached why Nya was excluded from this conversation. But shouldn't you be talking to Wendell and Nya?"

"I am, but he looks to you for support. I just want you to be available when he wants to talk."

AFTER WEBBER HAD LEFT the table, something she said kept buzzing in his head. Better insurance.

Chapter Five: The Mother In Law

In a recent case of mistaken identity, Lavon's younger brother Lovester had been shot. Lovester had been recovering well and decided to join Lavon for a morning walk/run. When the two men returned to the semi-mansion, they noticed a woman relaxing on one of the recliners. The woman was in her late sixties or early seventies. She wore a swimsuit that was better suited for a woman one-third her age—years of soft living oozed out from the swimsuit's bordering areas, exposing spotted and blemished skin.

"Good morning, ma'am." Lavon offered, hoping an explanation would come naturally.

"Oh, good, you must be the pool boy and the gardener. Good to see my daughter has had the good sense to start ordering help from a male stripper catalog." The woman eyed Lavon and Lovester.

At this point, Paden Dodd, Lynn's niece, walked from the main house, escorted by a middle-aged man. The man who escorted Paden looked familiar to Lavon, but not exactly. It was like he had seen an older version of this person.

Paden Dodd was the 24-year-old daughter of Constantine Dodd, a reputed underworld figure, and the Granddaughter of Dolan Dodd, an icon in the world of organized crime. Paden had a slight muscular frame that served well as a pro tennis player. Paden had stepped away from the tennis circuit without explanation. Paden had also appeared in some light roles in movies and television, mostly in shows that her family financially sponsored. Paden owned a restaurant called Paden's Place and Smoke House, popular in Shepherd's Pass. Recently, Paden began singing with Lovester Tyler, one of Lavon's younger brothers, at the restaurant. Lovester had stepped in front of a bullet meant for Padan, and she had begun to develop a romantic interest in Lovester, who still seemed to be hung up on a former girlfriend.

Paden Dodd was also the biggest supporter of happiness for Lynn Dodd-Masterson. Paden could read Lynn well enough to know her feelings were genuine for Lavon and, more importantly, reciprocated. Paden knew Lynn's first marriage had been a disaster and would not let this happen again.

"Barbara, no one wanted to look at your saggy ass forty years ago, so no one should have to look at it now. For the love of God, cover some of that up." As the man appeared bellowed, Lavon knew who he was. He had to be Constantine Dodd, the son of Lynn's uncle Dolan Dodd. Dolan Dodd was an underworld figure and reputed gangster; his son was reported to be even worse.

Paden giggled at her father's put down, ran to Lovester, and raised his shirt to check his wounds.

"Maybe the pool boy can get us fresh drinks," Barbara suggested.

Constantine looked at Lavon. "Do you see the kind of crap I have had to put up with? In a couple of days, you are becoming her son-in-law, and she can't tell you for a fucking pool boy."

"Watch your blood pressure, Daddy. Uncle Lavon is not offended." Paden stated in a sign-song voice clearly to irritate Barbara.

"If anyone is offended, it should be me. Your uncle Lavon cost me a quarter of a million dollars." Constantine stated.

"How?" Lavon was pulled into a need-to-know.

"Back when you played for the Florida State Seminoles, you played in a game and won."

"So."

"So, Sonny, that was during the academic cheating scandal."

"I was not at the school when that took place."

"Right, now try to follow along. Half the regular players were pulled and not allowed to play. So, I placed a small wager that the team would lose since any scrubs they could find on that short notice would not only be no good but would not have time to learn the system."

"I am sorry that I disappointed you by doing my best. And you are Constantine Dodd. Is that correct?"

"Yeah, that's me."

"Try to get your father and aunt to come to the wedding. I know he doesn't like being in the same room as the mayor, but this is special." Lavon's request seemed to startle Constantine.

"Who is your date for the wedding? Paden, are you taking that charming English guy who was following you around Hollywood?" Barbara asked.

"I am going with Lovester."

"Well, yes, dear, to sing a song or two, but I mean as a real date. There may be photographers and news people there. Who you are seen with is the key to success in the business."

"Barbara, if Lovester will have me as a real date, I want to go with him."

"Connie, talk to her."

"Sorry, Barbara, I am with my kid on this one. A guy steps in front of a bullet to keep her alive. If she wants to dance a couple of dances with him. In front of his family and ours, I am all for it."

WHEN LAVON ARRIVED at the police station, he was sure he would have a moment to catch his breath after the strange encounter with invading future relatives, but he was so wrong. Abby had located Leona Balboa at the car dealership where she worked, and Abby had been told Leona was there and available to speak to them. Leona Balboa led Lavon and Abby into a small cubical area that looked one-third the size it should be. Leona worked for Shepherd Pass Major Motors as a sales associate. Leona was a beautiful woman of Hispanic descent in her mid-twenties. Leona wore an impeccable women's three-piece business suit accentuated with a gold necklace and bangles for her wrist. Leona also wore a large signage ring that was obviously the company symbol for sales excellence. Leona was the niece of Ramon Ortiz, one of the people who had died and whose name appeared on Fiona's list. Lavon and Abby were clear something illegal had happened. They were also equally sure that whatever had happened to cause Fiona's murder was still going on. However, in police work, it is often not enough just knowing there is a crime afoot; investigators need to be able to articulate their findings. Lavon and Abby had to wait to get time with Leona because Leona was not only a sales associate, but also multilingual, and her services were needed outside of her own sales. Leona's small workspace looked like the anteroom for an accurate worker's space. Still, it was clear Leona had a sense of organization. Everything in the space seemed to be labeled, color-coded, and numbered.

"Well, it is not every day I get pulled off the sales floor for a visit from the royal family." Leona began as Lavon and Abby were seated.

In equal amazement, Lavon and Abby stared at each other.

"I think she means you." Abby finally offered.

"Couldn't be," Lavon responded.

"Look, I am sorry if I spoke out of turn. Everyone knows Dolan Dodd and his family own this dealership. A couple of months back, I was at Paden's Place, the smokehouse restaurant, and I heard her calling you Uncle something or other. If there is something I have deduced that is not something I am supposed to know, I can forget things easily."

"We are detectives, and we came here to ask a few follow-up questions about your uncle," Lavon stated.

Leona's eyes went wide, followed by sadness. "He was an old man, and he was no threat to you people. He ran his mouth a little, but that was all bluster. He still liked women in his later years."

"Look, I don't know about my partner, but I have had all the calling us gangsters I can deal with for one day," Abby stated.

"Ma'am, your uncle's death was listed as an accident. Are you telling us you think there was more to it than that?" Lavon attempted to redirect.

"They say my uncle fell off a ladder. Only my uncle never climbed ladders. He had vertigo. The only reason the ladder was there was for me to use when I came over to do household projects for him."

"And you told the police that investigated this?" Abby asked.

"I did. I also told that little black girl that came by asking." Leona explained.

"What little black girl?" Lavon asked.

"Her name was Fiona. I only remember because it rhymes with my name."

Lavon and Abby sat briefly while listening to Leona talk about her uncle and how proud he had been of her. Lavon and Abby knew they had collected all the information they needed from Leona. Still, they wanted to let her express her loss.

"I am going to get you one of those slick-looking suits the gangsters wear in the movies," Abby joked as she and Lavon left the dealership.

Abby had called most of the names on the list and was told by the people at those numbers that everyone on the list worked as a consultant for McIntosh Manufacturing, the same as the deceased people from the list.

"Look, Homer, I told you that if you need time to catch your breath after a morning encounter with a guest invasion, I can handle this. It is probably nothing at all." Abby stated as she and Lavon entered McIntosh Manufacturing. The McIntosh building was a mammoth structure that covered a half mile of buildings and storage sheds. Inside the main building was a collection of large multicolored pipes running in all directions. There were rows of machines punching, pressing, blow molding, compression molding, excursion molding, vulcanizing, and processing the inner guts of who knows what machines. Workers rushed in all directions in multicolored smocks with head and show covering. The workers were at least 90 percent Black, Hispanic or Asian. "I think we died and went to the U.N.," Abby commented.

"It is just a lot to take in all at once," Lavon admitted.

"I used to love your mother-in-law's bra commercials."

"If that is a joke, it is not even slightly funny. I just saw her in a bathing suit." Lavon shook his head like he was to shake an ugly image loose that was lodged for the duration.

"Okay, so she used to be an actress. Back when the gangsters flooded Vegas and started funding movies in Hollywood. Then she did some commercials and finally dropped to appearing on a soap opera."

Lavon and Abby agreed to start in human resources. The plan was to have the human resources director pull the individuals from the list and find out what they did. So far, the same ten people worked for the same place and went in a group to the gym, and coincidence was wearing thin.

As Lavon and Abby walked toward the sign that read Human Resources, a humongous man started staring at them. The man was over six feet tall and weighed over 400 lbs. His big scraggly beard stuck through his beard cover.

Abby reached into her purse and pulled out the picture Visionary had drawn for them to show Lavon. Visionary had managed to capture the angry eyes of the giant captured perfectly. Before Lavon could look up from the picture, the giant had tackled him full-on, and Lavon went sailing through the air and landed in a row of rolling toolboxes. Lavon then slides backward in a spill of cutting oil. Abby grabbed a pipe that was leaning against the wall. The giant turned around and reached for Abby. She ducked underneath and hit the giant as hard as she could on the chin. The giant screamed, and before he could reconcile the pain, Lavon hit him with a flying tackle. It took a significant wrestling match to get the giant cuffed. Lavon had to cuff one hand while Abby cuffed the other, and then the duo cuffed the two sets of handcuffs together to secure the giant's hands behind his back.

"Find your phone and call a squad car to transport," Lavon instructed Abby.

"You mean call a tow truck for this fat bastard," Abby grumbled.

"I want a lawyer." The giant cried out.

"You need a dietician and a team of personal trainers working around the clock. Bitch. Shut the fuck up." Abby replied. "And God am I glad you did not let me come here by myself, Tyler."

"SORRY, I MISSED THE festivities. It looks like you both had fun." After the uniformed officers carted off Borland Fischer, the giant who wrestled with Lavon and Abby, they sat in Ms. Parnell's human resources office. Abby had ripped another jacket, and her hair was such a mess that she decided not to try to fix it. Lavon and Abby had visible bruises but wore them like victory badges. Lavon was obviously roughed up, but he was recovering quickly.

"Look, we just came here to ask a few questions." Abby began.

"I understand, but we cannot divulge or share any records with you without approval from our legal counsel."

"Look, lady, I am not asking you to divulge anything like the secret to what goes in the secret sauce. I just want a little information on the giant that I just wrestled with." Abby gripped.

"Well, ma'am, judging from your appearance, I would not be surprised to find out that wrestling with large men was a habit of yours," Parnell stated.

Abby was about to say something, but Lavon stopped her. "You are right, Ms. Parnell. You see, my partner gets a little worked up at times.

I did not want to get a warrant because we were unsure, we were at the right place. Now, considering events or, as you say, festivities, we know we are. So, we are going to get a court order for all paperwork in this building. That will include the paper you use to wipe your ass." Lavon stood and reached for Abby's hand to assist her in standing.

"Wait, you are talking about shutting down production while a bunch of bureaucrats go over information, they may never be able to understand. I could take weeks, and we would miss deadlines and contract obligations."

"What is more important, Ms. Parnell, is that when your corporate offices find out you could have avoided this but instead chose to have a pissing contest with my partner, what do you think they will do with you."

"WERE YOU REALLY WILLING to tie this company up?" Abby asked Lavon. They had been given the fills for the ten workers in question and the files for Borland Fischer. The two sat in a small, unventilated office, reviewing what they had been given.

"Oh yes. I think there isn't a judge in his right mind that would not let me freeze this company until I got back from my honeymoon after we were attacked." Lavon sat staring at the calendar on the wall of the office. The calendar was from Mount Rushmore Insurance Company. Lavon began riffling through papers quickly. "Didn't you tell me Alisa's grandmother only had one insurance company?"

"Yes, the guy we went to visit."

"Then why are there payments to Mount Rushmore Insurance in her folder?"

Abby began checking, and all ten folders listed Mount Rushmore Insurance Company. "They all have it."

"I know what is going on, but I need to collect some more information. In the meantime, don't let anyone know we know what is going on."

"Hey, hillbilly brain, we don't."

LAVON AND ABBY SAT in the court office, Duckworth in front of them and Raintree with his back to the room.

"Since you called this meeting, why don't you begin, Detective Tyler." Duckworth opened.

"We need your help, and you are going to help us." Lavon's statement caused Raintree to turn and face the room.

"Are you here to confess to inappropriate conduct?" Raintree asked.

"No, we are here because we have a crime resulting in multiple murders. We can arrest the people on our level, but we have every reason to believe that the murders were a part of the corporate plan. When we arrest the people, we are going to arrest tomorrow. We know the corporate board will start shredding documents, and the fat cats on the top get away as usual." Lavon explained.

"That is unless you help or send us in the right direction," Abby added.

"Let me get this straight: You have a national case, but you can't handle it alone?" Duckworth asked.

"Exactly," Lavon confirmed.

"But you did not go to the F.B.I.?" Raintree asked.

"No, but if you tell me that is where I should be, I will go there. But the D.O.J. is over the F.B.I., and it is your call." Lavon outlined.

"See, we do not want to be accused of doing an end run around whatever you guys are working on," Abby said.

"What are you asking in return for this gesture?" Duckworth asked.

"Only that you listen. We will outline what we know and how we know it. If, for some reason, you don't want to be involved, no problem," Lavon explained.

"This sounds too good to be true," Raintree responded.

"Not really. My partner knows that if we have to form some task force, he could miss his wedding or the honeymoon. And all you guys have to do is hear us out," Abby offered.

Lavon smiled, not because he knew he had trapped Duckworth and Raintree with an offer they could not refuse. The smile was more because Lavon could feel he and Abby were clicking the way he had always planned they could.

Chapter Six: The Day of the Arrests

It was Friday, the day before Lavon's bachelor party and two days before the wedding. Lavon and Abby were back at Arron Flack's home. Arron looked a little less emotionally worn than before, but it was still obvious that he was hurting at the loss of his younger sister.

"We have some news; Aaron and I don't know how you are going to take it, so let me explain as much as I can." Lavon began.

"Aaron, we feel we have caught the man that killed your sister. We believe that he has killed at least three other people and maybe a whole lot more." Abby filed in.

"Then that is good."

'Well, Aaron, we have a witness for one of the murders and an artist who drew a sketch of him that helped identify the killer." Lavon explained.

"So, what is the problem," Aaron asked.

"We believe that he murdered them under orders from the company he works for."

"That's stupid. Why?" Aaron asked.

"Key man insurance. Let me explain. The original idea was that let's say, a group of people start a business. Each partner has their area of specialty. The guy that does the accounting, for example, dies. The other partners need to cover his specialty with a replacement until a permanent solution can be found. So, the insurance covers the loss of revenue during the transition." Lavon began explaining.

Aaron looked confused.

"Aaron, the company kept their retired employees as consultants. Paid for their gym memberships and gave them a token salary. To let them sit around in the break room two days a week and talk about the old times." Abby filled in.

"Then, when the company needed a cash influx, it had someone go out and harvest the crop. We located a separate 1.9-million-dollar policy on Garcia with the company named as the beneficiary that her family did not know about." Lavon explained.

Aaron's eyes went wide. He now knew what they were explaining. "And my brat ass sister put it together when she became friends with Garcia."

"So, what's the problem? The guy is a killer. Arrest him."

"We did. And by the way, sumo wrestling is not a part of police training. I lost another jacket and ripped a bra strap. Funny, they never tell you in those bullshit cop TV shows you keep having to fight so hard you are always out searching for new underwear."

Arron chuckled slightly. "Detective Blackwell, you are covered."

"Here are the issues. We may not have him for your sister's murder since the only witness in that alley was intoxicated at the time. The murders were falsely signed off as accidental, which means a cop, or cops need to be dealt with. And the federal agents may need to dismantle that company." Abby outlined.

"But my sister not only helped you find a mass murderer but helped to prevent countless deaths in the future, is that right?"

"Yes, that is how I see it," Lavon answered.

"Then I can only feel glad that she died doing what she loved most of all: protecting other people and not letting smart criminals escape through the cracks." Aaron then turned to Abby. "Blackwell, I know we have had our issues over the years, but you did your job when it came down to it. I know that because you look like you went ten rounds with Big Foot."

"I did the grungy bearded bastard."

"HI ZEB, GOOD TO SEE you. Still wearing that awful toupee," Abby greeted as she entered Zeb's Magic Touch. Zeb Gunderson was a retired Shepherds Pass detective. He was a pale reflection of a handsome man living within the remaining shell. He wore a thick clump of a toupee and smiled through ill-fitting false teeth.

Lavon and Abby entered Zeb's salon with Sergeant Wendell Bishop and Officer Webber.

"Double date, huh," Zeb commented, looking over his shoulder. He had an elderly woman in his salon chair in the process of turning her grey hair into some non-human pastel.

"Zeb Gunderson, we have a warrant for your arrest," Lavon informed.

"Bullshit. Let me see it." Zeb took the warrant and examined it quickly. "This is federal."

"I told you he could read," Abby commented to the group.

"Why the hell is a local cop handing out federal paper?"

"It is simple, Zeb, baby. Your local crimes lead to a federal crime, so the Feds want you too. Our judge is busy even as we speak drafting separate charges."

"You clowns are trying to do an end run around the 1970 RICO or the 2024 change. That is unconstitutional."

"You want to talk about the Constitution, Zeb. Let's talk. The Constitution says that if there is a conflict in law that is local, city, or state, then Federal Law takes precedence. That means they get you first, and if you live long enough, we get you, so the judge drafting local charges has twenty years to do it."

"The good cops you work with will crucify you, and you know it."

"Not when they find out you purchased this place with a check from the manufacturing company that ordered its employees murdered," Abby explained.

"So, I did a favor and listed a few old nobodies as accidents. What was the harm."

The old lady Zeb was dying, jumped up and ran from the room still wearing the smock she had been cover in for the dye job.

"Income tax evasion to the fed. We have four counts of murder and seven conspiracies to commit. Now, Bishop and Webber, if you will do the honors of hooking this guy up, we have others to visit." Lavon instructed.

"SO, WHAT IS THIS TREND toward co-ed bachelor parties all about?" Abby asked Wendell. Wendell recently married Nya, and Webber has sponsored his co-ep bachelor's party. Now, Wendell and Webber were in charge of Lavon's bachelor's party, which was also scheduled to be co-ep. Lavon and Abby sat with Wendell and Webber in an interrogation room, waiting for the guards to escort Borland Fischer and his legal representative to the room.

"When half the people you work with are female, to exclude them from the fun side of things when they support you every other day is like slapping them in the face," Wendell explained.

"Besides, the female presence helps the humor keep from getting too raunchy," Webber added.

Three guards led Borland Fischer's hulking frame in. The expression on Borland's guard broadcasted the trouble Borland had been in thus far. Borland was chained to a steel table, and a small man in wire-rim glasses spoke. "I am Donald Owens, counsel for Mr. Fischer, and you people have wasted enough of our time. I was told arraignment was being held until you civil servants arrived."

"Hi, teddy bear, how's the leg?" Abby taunted.

Borland looked at Abby and sneered.

"This is a police misconduct case if ever I have seen one," Owens claimed.

"The giant attacked two cops." Abby shrieked.

"And how was he to know you were cops?" Owens asked.

"So, it is alright for a 400-pound man to tackle an average citizen. Where did you go to school again?" Lavon asked.

"Sounds more like a misunderstanding." Owens concocted.

"Good try. But we did not come here to discuss the assault. We came here to add additional charges. Four counts of murder and seven counts of conspiracy to commit murder, for starters." Lavon explained.

"Wait, what are you talking about?" Owens asked, genuinely confused.

"Since you are in a lethal injection state, you may want your client to bring you up to speed on the murder-for-hire business," Abby stated.

"I obviously need time to talk with my client." Owens offered.

"Take your time; our work here is done. But in less than an hour, the feds are coming for a visit, and they won't be as nice as us," Abby said.

Lavon looked at Wendell and Webber, who seemed to enjoy the show. "Alright, now it's time for you guys to help us with the really hard part," Lavon stated, and they began walking through the door.

"What did he just say?" Wendell asked Abby.

Abby just shrugged and smiled.

DETECTIVE IVY HAD NOW joined Lavon and Abby and Wendell and Webber. Detective Ivy is a rail-thin black detective who works officer-involved shootings and internal affairs for Shepherds Pass. Ivy went into Detective Don Nash's office and spent a few minutes. Then Don Nash exited the office, and Ivy took his seat.

"No cleaner way to do this, I suppose," Nash asked Lavon as he approached.

"Clean has not been the order of the day, boss," Lavon answered.

Nash led the small group to Officer O'Leary's desk. "Detective O'Leary, I am requesting that you remove your badge and gun and go to my office at this time."

Through the window of Don Nash's office, O'Leary could see Ivy seated behind the desk in Nash's office.

"What the fuck is this some kind of joke?"

"No joke, detective, you are at this moment temporally suspended. And Ivy would like a word with you."

"All this trouble is over this rancid piece of ass you wouldn't even stick your dick in," O'Leary mumbled. He pushed past Lavon and headed for Nash's office, muttering incoherent curse words.

"That wasn't too bad," Wendell observed. No sooner had the words left him than they could see O'Leary had bounded over the desk and begun trying to strangle Ivy.

"Go. Go. Go." Nash cried out, and Webber and Wendell took off to rescue Ivy. Abby also tried to run, but Lavon grabbed her arm, holding her back. "Enough wrestling for you for one-week, young lady."

"God, do you know you are even more fuck up than I am in your own way?" Abby laughed.

"So, are you coming to the wedding?"

"What is Bobby Joe's favorite color."

"I think he likes seeing a woman in a delicate color like peach Are you going to buy a new dress?"

"No, a bra and matching thong. I think I got off on the wrong foot with your sister Jody, and I might need to bribe him to keep her from beating me to death."

As Wendell and Webber led O'Leary out of the office in handcuffs, Abby called out, "What a shame you guys are going to miss our grand finally for the evening."

"GOOD EVENING, MS. PARNELL. You are looking lovelier than ever today." Lavon and Abby had returned to McIntosh Manufacturing. This time, they were with Prosecutor Raintree, D.O.J. Duckworth, Tim Patterson of the F.B.I., and about twenty of Tim Patterson's agents from the local F.B.I. office.

"What the hell is this?" Parnell sneered.

"Well, I promised these guys a little introduction. This is Mr. Raintree with the Federal Prosecutors office, and this is Duckworth with D.O.J. Just as importantly, this is a new friend of mine, Tim Patterson, with the F.B.I."

"No, you country-sounding moron, what are all these people doing here?"

"Well, ma'am, I think the Prosecutor will explain."

"Ma'am I have a lawful cease and desist order signed by a federal judge. You will, at this time, stop all manufacturing practices. A member of the F.B.I. will hand you a box. You will fill the box only with your personal items, and you will be escorted from the property and told to line up across the street. You will await further instructions. Your entire workforce will also comply with these rules. If you try to destroy, shred, or alter any document or item on these premises, you will be arrested and made to answer to the fullest extent of the law. If you try to reenter the building before written notice has been given to you, you will be arrested. Do you understand?"

"Yes, I understand. The police came here to push us around, and we pushed back a little, and they went and called the Gestapo."

"That is close enough for me," Duckworth commented, then turned to Patterson. "Have your people clear the building and box every scrap of paper they find."

"He warned you about saving some toilet paper," Abby whispered to Parnell.

"You are kicking over a hornet's nest. You have no idea who is involved in this company." Parnell.

"You see, that is where you are wrong. I am coordinating operations just like this to all your branches as well as the insurance company that sponsored this little Machiavellian tragedy." Raintree stated. Something in this form of dismantling of an organization seemed to energize him.

"MY SISTERS ARE IN TOWN, and I have not had time to spend with them. I think I am going to go find them and give them a hard time." Lavon stated to Abby.

"It will have to wait. Your sisters and your soon-to-be wife went on a girl's shopping spree with my wife. I think the Shepherds Pass economy is about to double, and I think I am headed for the poorhouse," Tim Patterson said as he overheard Lavon.

Chapter Boot Seven: Scooting Hoedown

It was now Saturday, the day of Lavon's bachelor's party. Lavon knew the only way he could take off work and spend a week away for his honeymoon was to come in today and assist Abby with the paperwork that complied with the case they had rushed through this week. That Wendell and Webber had chosen for Lavon's bachelor party was a Hillbilly Hoedown. All the guys coming were to dress in plaid shirts and jeans, and the women attending were to wear matching stereotypical country outfits. Lavon now sat across from Abby; Lavon wore a plaid shirt, jeans, and boots.

"I thought I might find the both of you here." Lavon and Abby peeked up from their paperwork mountains and saw it was Duckworth in another of his ill-fitting suits.

"Good morning, Mr. Duckworth. Did you come to add to the avalanche of paperwork?" Abby asked in a sarcastic tone.

"No, I can give you two a sort of unofficial report on what we found during our raids on both McIntosh and Mount Rushmore insurance."

"Unofficial." Abby queried.

"Yeah, unofficial because there is no way the Fed wants us to know as much as them," Lavon stated.

"Look, to be perfectly honest, there is some truth to that. Anytime you compile this much data, there is a lot of stuff to sort out, and figuring out what is a part of the crime and what is coincidental data captured in the net takes time." Duckworth revealed. "I also want to pick your brains since you guys put this together so fast you probably had a theory on what we are seeing."

"Where is Raintree? Is this his day to shave his legs?" Abby asked.

"Don't worry about Raintree, Abby. I understand where he was coming from. And to some degree, he made a good observation." Lavon stated.

Duckworth took a seat, and he and Abby stared at Lavon, knowing that Lavon would tell them more.

"About five years ago, I was working as a State cop in Mississippi, and there was this girl that had been dating this horrible piece of shit that had been locked up for three or four years. During that time, the girl saw the light. She started going to church and helping out in volunteer activities. She worked with rescue animals and found a job as a checker in the local store." Lavon began his story.

"So, happy ending, right?" Duckworth asked.

"The guy got out of prison, and the next thing you know, the girl is in the hospital in a coma. She had been beaten up so bad we didn't know if she would ever come out of it, and there is some question as to whether any memory of what all transpired would be salvageable."

"Did you arrest the boyfriend and send him back where he belongs?" Abby was now pulled into the story.

"No, remember I was a state detective. One of the local cops went to question the boyfriend. The boyfriend smarted off to the cop, and the cop shot the guy while he was in handcuffs and in front of witnesses."

"Jesus, this is a horrible story," Duckworth complained.

"Don't worry, it gets worse. I got there to arrest the cop. It turns out the cop would rather die than go to prison with the people he sent there. So, the cop committed suicide. Six months later, the girlfriend that was beaten comes out of her coma. She has memory and tells us the boyfriend never touched her. The boyfriend's sister and a group of her girl pals beat the shit out of her."

"So somewhere along the way, I missed the point out," Duckworth confessed.

"The point is everyone did what they thought they should based on the information they had led them. But the conclusion they arrived at was wrong." Abby clarified. "My partner is telling you that he has occasionally been offered deals and higher-paying jobs with strings attached, but he has never even considered taking them. And he understands why the Raintrees of the world are suspicious of him."

"And I don't blame them. So, how did your raids go unofficially." Lavon attempted to lighten the conversation.

"Well, tons of information has been collected. Since you like stories, here is a short one. About ten years ago, an Ivy League professor released a study showing the names of a large group of U.S.-based businesses that are extremely wealthy, and their competitors may never be able to catch up. The wealth of the companies on that list came from U.S. Slavery and was built on the backs of black people. Now, that ends that part of my story. McIntosh was built on the dead bodies of immigrants and illegal aliens who could barely understand English, let alone understand the complicated legal jargon they were asked to sign. Hundreds of millions of dollars have changed hands from Rushmore to McIntosh over the years. Anytime there is a financial downturn in the economy, some poor immigrant dies, and there is a cash influx to McIntosh."

"Sounds straightforward, so what's the problem?" Abby asked.

"The problem is we need the key. What linked these companies, and which one is the parasite, and which is really the host." Duckworth sat back.

"Well, if this were our case, I would be looking for someone who has worked in both companies in the past or who has a spouse or significant other who works for the other company. You see, U.S. companies are not cookie-cutter or one-size-fits-all. You are looking for someone who knows or has access to the inner workings of both companies," Lavon offered.

"And everyone else is dancing like puppets on a string." Duckworth saw the point.

"And speaking of dancing. You will have to find a plaid shirt and jeans, or you will stand out during the square-dancing tonight." Lavon stated.

"What is he saying now?" Duckworth looked at Abby.

"He is saying you have to come to his bachelor party as payment for his help."

ABBY HAD THE THREESOME stop by a resale shop she knew. Duckworth found a plaid shirt and jeans that surprisingly fit him better than the business suit he had been wearing. Abby also found a sports coat she liked to replace one recently destroyed in the line of duty.

"Hey Bobby Joe, I want you to meet......"

But before Lavon could complete the introduction, his older brother grabbed Abby and passionately kissed her. The banquet room for the bachelor party was decked out in the theme of a country hoedown. In the past, Lavon complained that most people in Shepherds Pass had no idea what the difference was between a cowboy and a plowboy. So, country and Western themes have been deliberately thrown together to irritate the guest of honor. There were over fifty guests by the time Lavon and Abby arrived. The crowd broke into cheers when Bobby Joe grabbed and kissed Abby. "That is for saving my little brother's ass time and time again." Bobby Joe stated. Bobby Joe Tyler is slightly taller and more muscular than Lavon. Bobby Joe seemed to be releasing Abby, who now sported a totally befuddled and dazed look on her face, and he grabbed and kissed her again. "And that for not making me have to dance the couples dance tomorrow with my baby sister."

"Take it easy, bro," Lavon commented.

"Sorry, kid, you had your chance." Bobby Joe retorted.

"Yeah, sorry, kid, you had your chance." Abby incoherently murmured.

"Why don't I find a nice corner for us to get to know each other, and I can teach you the moves you need for tonight's square dance." Bobby Joe led Abby off.

"Hey, lady, do you want me to call a cop?" Barney asked Abby. "Oh, that's right; you are a cop." The crowd began to cheer even louder.

Wendell and Webber rushed over to Lavon and Duckworth. "Good, you are right on time," Webber told Duckworth.

"I am sorry for the aggressive questioning today," Duckworth started. "And if even I didn't know I was going to end up here, how could I be right on time?"

"Well, sir, there are two rules today. Number one, no business, and number two, no bullshit." Wendell informed Duckworth. Wendell showed Duckworth a clipboard he was carrying. "See, I got you scheduled for the axe-throwing competition."

Duckworth looked at the clipboard. "Wait, that says Unsuspecting Sucker."

"Well, we had to fill the competition," Webber added, handing Lavon and Duckworth bottles of beer from a passing server. Wendell and Webber were dressed in identical Western outfits to show that they were the event hosts.

"What about his brother Bobby Joe and all those guys over there?" Duckworth asked.

"They are firemen, which means, for all we know, they sleep with an axe under their pillow," Webber explained and laughed.

"I must be losing my mind, but that almost makes sense." But before Duckworth could rethink anything, he saw someone he knew. "Wait, I thought you said you don't know Andrew Tyler from the D.O.J.?"

"I don't," Lavon confirmed.

"Well, that is funny because he is walking this way."

"Hey, Duckworth, how is your investigation going?" Andrew asked a befuddled Duckworth.

"Strange," Duckworth answered. "And it keeps getting stranger."

"I am Andrew Tyler. I am sorry to crash your bachelor party, but Anita and Noreen dropped me off here and told me I should meet you while they are at the bridal shower." Andrew shook Lavon's hand.

"Nice grip. I guess little league pitching will do that." Lavon assumed.

Duckworth was led off to prepare for the axe throw.

"So, you are the one with a sister named Lindsey." Lavon further assessed.

"Yes, and I also came to apologize if she has made herself a pest. She is my mother's assistant campaign manager. She is sure that since my mother is a Senator. We are wealthy, but my sister is afraid some woman with low ethical standards will try to invade the family."

Lavon finished his beer and then grabbed another for Andrew and himself. "You know I would be offended at the low standards part of that explanation if I did not have seven sisters who always think they need to protect us guys from ourselves."

"I don't know your sister that well, but I thought since I never do anything spontaneous, this would give me points for being human," Andrew stated, gulping his beer.

"Well, it is a no business night, and you look like a guy that can throw an axe."

"What?"

DUCKWORTH DID POORLY in the axe-throwing contest, much to the delight of the firefighters who were judges. The fireman judges offered him a chance to redeem himself by participating in the assisted pie-eating contest. When Lavon inquired as to what an assisted pie eating contest was, a group of officers grabbed him, Duckworth, and the others Wendell had designated to participate and handcuff them and sat them at a table. The pie-eating contestants were forced feed pie for the duration of the contest. Since they had no access to their hands, they had to cry out for Mother's milk, please. One of the female officers would give them milk by allowing them to suck it from a balloon that was shaped like a woman's breast.

THE SQUARE DANCING was the high point of the evening. Even people who did not feel they could creatively dance were swept into the routine. Abby found Bobby to be a good teacher and enjoyed their dancing together.

"You Tyler boys, being so close in age, probably have had to compete against each other all your lives," Abby said to Bobby as they were catching their breaths from the square dancing.

"Yeah, I guess so." Bobby slowly answered as though he knew where her inquiry was headed.

"Kissing works better when you are not trying to upstage your brother or prove a point."

"Sorry."

"Don't be sorry, but the next time we kiss, I want to know it is because you want to kiss me."

"Then, are we still good for the wedding dance?"

"Bobby Joe Tyler, there is no one on this planet I would rather be dancing with," Abby answered.

LAVON TYLER HAD PLAYED college football at Florida State and then enlisted in the Army. Since Lavon had spent so much time as an athlete, he did not drink much; this evening, however, Wedell and Webber made it a point to keep plying him with liquor.

"Excuse me, but we have not met yet, and you being the guest of honor, I don't want to appear rude. My name is Wade Vaughn, and I am with the Mississippi Bureau of Investigation. In fact, I think I have your old job." Wade Vaughn was Lavon's sister Jody's newest partner in the M.B.I. He was a man with a ruggedly handsome look and a scar on his chin that touched his mouth.

Lavon struggled to focus. "Came a long way to suck milk. But I hope you like being a Mississippi State Detective; I sure did."

"Yes, that too. But by your other old job, I mean looking out for Jody when she gets upset or frustrated. See, I am her new partner."

Lavon motioned for Wade to step closer. "Let you in on a little secret."

"What's that?"

"She aint half as tough as she pretends to be."

Chapter Eight: The Bridal Shower

In the 1800s, a group of cattlemen involved in feuding with the local sheep herders blocked the main path to water and grassland from the herds of sheep. The sheepherders accepted that they were outnumbered and outgunned. They devised a secret pass to allow them a back door into the watering holes and the plentiful grassland. The secret area became known later as Shepherds Pass. No one at that time needed to put Shepherds Pass on a map lest war breaks out.

When Highway 70 was built, an off-ramp was constructed to allow people access to the ragged, dilapidated town that had now sprung up because the town offered two very vital things the area needed. First was a gas station that carried diesel fuel for the trucks that moved down the highway all night. And two if offered two all-night tow and auto repair shops. The repair shops were owned by the Dodd brothers, Leo and Raymond. As the country grew and its needs changed, so did the needs and tastes of the Dodd brothers. They became involved in gambling pro, prostitution, and bootlegging during the twenties. The sins of man rained, and because the off-the-road Truckstop grew into a small town.

At some point, the two Dodd brothers chose different paths. Leo Dodd married and started a family that fought hard to legitimize the existence of the family businesses. Leo Dodd's offspring sought education and philanthropy. Leo Dodd's children and their children would spend years after his death struggling to cleanse the family name.

Raymond Dodd and his children went the other path entirely. They believed in the ways of organized crime. They sought just as hard to excel in their felonious endeavors as the Children of Leo did in education and goodwill; due to a common beginning and the view from spectators from outside the family, they were destined always to overlap in the family's values and name.

Lynn Dodd-Masterson, Barbara Dodd's daughter, is most closely related to the Raymond Dodd side of the family. Dolan Dodd, Barbara's brother, is a widely known, reputed gangster who controls many illegal operations in and around Shepherds Pass. Lynn decided at an early age she would work to unify the family and to clean up as much of the bad family image as possible. To do this, she became a judge even though she had married a mob enforcer. Lynn's husband was murdered by one of her cousins in a fit of jealous rage and is currently doing time for that crime. Lynn's lack of loyalty to the organized crime side of the Dodd family had caused rifts between her and her mother; Barbara left Lynn to be raised by her aunt Joann and Rosa, their maid.

On his arrival in Shepherds Pass, Lynn had made the first overtures toward Lavon about six months ago. Lynn had originally misjudged Lavon's attempt to get a court order signed for a failed prank and insulted him. Now Lynn stood in the study of her semi-mansion, opening bridal gifts from Lavon's mother and sisters.

"Alright Lynn that nighty has a no return policy. So does my brother, so once you walk him down the aisle, aint no giving him back." Jody joked. Jody is a state detective with the Mississippi Bureau of Investigation. Jody had worked some cases with her brother Lavon while working in the M.B.I. Jody had introduced Casey, Lavon's former fiancée to him. When Casey turns out to be unfaithful, Jody fears a serious riff with her brother may occur. Knowing Lavon was happy again, being here for Lynn's bridal shower made her happy. Jody brought Wade Vaughn, her new partner, and his daughter Sabrina to Shepherds Pass for the wedding.

"Maybe you should rethink this, Lynn. I have kissed a lot of frogs in my day, and none of them have turned into princes. I have kissed my fair share of princes, and some have reverted back to being frogs." Barbara boasted from behind a large tumbler of Pettibone brandy.

"Just for the record Barbara. I have seven sons, and they have a tendency to be knuckleheads and daredevils. Sometimes, they think it is their responsibility to save the world. They come by that honestly because their father has always been that way. But at no point had any of my boys been subject to turning into a frog." Rebecca Tyler declared.

Rebecca's comment caused Paden Dodd to laugh.

The women sat in a helter-skelter arrangement in the mists of a pile of boxes, all decorated and addressed to Lynn.

"Alright, running back, this one is from me." Anita Tyler handed a small package to Lynn. "This is a cologne guaranteed to get me more nieces and nephews. I gave the same stuff to Alice; Norbert's wife and she is working on child number seven."

"Oh my God, is whatever that is even legal?" Barbara slurred.

"Speaking of spreading the Tyler love, what is happening with you and Lovester?" Anita turned her attention to Paden.

Among the Tyler girls, Anita Tyler was known to be quick-witted and, at times, daring. This combination made Anita an excellent quarterback for charity football games. Norbert, Anita's oldest brother, taught Anita to quarterback with the best of them. Norbert had been an excellent quarterback in high school and college but never considered going professional. His love was his high school sweetheart, and building a family was Norbert's preferred path in life. Norbert owned a small auto repair shop in Lamont, Mississippi.

Anita's second passion was poker. Anita had learned to be great at poker through deception. She had been good at masking how well she absorbed the lessons taught when playing against other players. Anita could read tells so well in others that sometimes it looked like mine reading. Many of the Tyler children and taken a family oath to help others and to be of service to the country that had provided so much for their family. Anita was in the U.S.U.S. Army but was recently assigned to a project with the F.B.I. Anita knew her father had orchestrated this assignment through his varied contacts but did not mention it to anyone. Anita was now enrolled in the F.B.I. academy and set to work with Waldron Clarkson, Senior Supervisory Special Agent for the F.B.I. as soon as she graduates.

Anita's romantic life, if it could be called that, lacked fanfare. She had never lost the desire to be the star in a storybook romance but had not been settled in one place long enough for that to transpire. Independent, smart-mouthed, quick-witted football and poker-playing women did not seem to her to be in high demand. Besides being good at football and poker, Anita was better at a couple of things many men felt they dominated by default.

"For god's sake, don't give her any of that magic baby stuff." Barbara knocked back another slug of the brandy.

"Lovester and I have not been doing any baby making stuff, Barbara. We are friends and I really love singing with him."

"I hate it when you call me that. Why don't you show me the same respect you show other people?" Barbara complained.

"I agreed to take Eric to the wedding tomorrow." Noreen attempted to redirect the flow of the conversation. "He is super smart but a little shy."

"Who are you dancing with, Jody?" Lynn asked.

"Detective Wade Vaughn. He is my new partner. He is handsome. He is in the process of getting a divorce." Jody answered.

"Remember my rule one. Don't give him the thing until he loses the other woman's ring." Barbara stated.

Lynn and all the Tyler women stared at Barbara.

"Gee Barbara, you never seem to miss a chance to embarrass this family," Paden observed.

Sabrina, Detective Vaughn's fourteen-year-old deaf-mute daughter, had been watching, trying to lip-read enough to understand the conversations. Sabrina, in fact, took on a grim look. Sabrina had been sitting with Kim Tyler, Rebecca's 19-year-old daughter. Kim had experienced a soccer playing issue, and when Lynn visited Shepherds Pass, Lynn replaced Kim for the charity games.

Rebecca walked over to Sabrina and began signing to her and Sabrina started to smile at whatever Rebecca was telling her.

"Hold the phone, momma. I had no idea you could sign." Jody broadcasted.

"Well, when you are a teacher for over thirty years, they teach you more than just finger painting."

"So, Quarterback, tell us about your mystery man." Lynn prodded Anita.

"His name is Andrew Tyler. He is from a rich Tyler family that raised horses for racing down in South Carolina. I just found out his mother is a Senator."

"Where did you meet him?" Noreen asked. Noreen Tyler had recently graduated from law school in St. Louis and had passed the bar exam. She currently works as an intern for a full-service law firm.

"I was working for Waldron Clarkson, and they mixed Andrew's, and my name tags up at a meeting."

"You work for who?" A shocked look overcame Rebecca Tyler.

"Well, I am on loan to the F.B.I. and am slated to go to the F.B.I. academy. Andrew is with the Department of Justice."

"That dirty rat." Rebecca sneered.

"Which rat, momma?" Jody asked.

"Your father. And as soon as I find him, I am going to give him a piece of my mind. Because the bit he is working off needs all the help it can get. How dare that man give one of my girls to that adulterer."

"Technically momma he did not give me to him he loaned be to him." Anita tried to correct but it failed miserably.

Chapter Nine: The Day of the Wedding

Lavon awakened, reaching for Lynn as he had done so many mornings before. She was not there. Lavon struggle to rise from the lethargy known as sleep to recall the night that had passed. The room was too bright, and the bed too small. For a moment Lavon begun to wonder if he was still sleeping. Maybe he was still dreaming and had he somehow been caught in the Goldie Locks tale. Lavon lived in Lynn's Semi Mansion. Lynn had moved him there without his permission since he was in a coma caused by a drug reaction following treatment for a fight in an attempt to arrest a suspect. Shortly after that, Nya, the wife of one of his best friends in Shepherds Pass, had come up missing. Lavon realized how comforting it was to awaken with someone beside you who truly loves you.

Slowly, Lavon's memory began to reconstruct. The bachelor party had been the night before and he had drunk more than usual since he felt obligated to drink with most of the guest at some point.

He was in the Wendell's house. Now he remembered he had promised to abide by Lynn's wish that Lavon not see her the wedding day before she is led to the altar. He had planned to spend the night in Wendell's guest room, but the room he woke up in was the room they were converting into a nursery for the baby on the way. Nya and Wendell did not want to know the sex of the baby before the delivery, so the room was painted a pale neutral green. There was a baby bed and the small child's bed that he woke up on.

"Good you are awake. Wendell will return soon. He went to get something for you. Please remove your shirt." Nya requested as Wendell walked to the Bishop's kitchen. There was something in Nya's tone that was concerning, but he had not been awake long enough to ascertain why her mood seemed to be adversarial.

"Nya, If I said or did anything while I was drunk or caused Wendell to misbehave, you have my heartfelt apologies."

"Take off your shirt and sit in the chair," Nya instructed.

Reluctantly, Lavon did as instructed.

Once Lavon was seated, Nya covered him with a towel and poured rubbing alcohol into a shallow bowl. She then took out a leather strap and fastened one end to the handle of one of the kitchen drawers. At no time during her movement did she take her eyes off Lavon. Slowly, Nya reached into her apron pocket, took out a straight razor, and began smoothing the burs from the razor blade with quick, deliberate strokes.

"Right about now, Nya, you are starting to scare the hell out of me," Lavon confessed.

"Why?"

"Because you are wielding a straight razor."

"Women where I am from become proficient with a straight razor before they are ten."

"Would it be rude of me to ask what a ten-year-old girl is shaving?"

"Who said anything about shaving? I said we become proficient with them", Nya said, and she walked out to the room. Nya returned with a shaving mop and cup, mixing the lather. There was only the tapping of the side of the shaving brush against the cup as she stared at Lavon.

"Mr. Tyler, have you entered into a conspiracy against me?" Nya asked.

"Hell, no, Nya. We are friends."

Nya stared into Lavon's face as though everything she needed to know could be easily read. Nya began lathering Lavon's face. "My husband spoke to me about the possibility of having a child with Shelia, Webber's wife." There was a sharper bit to Nya's tone than Lavon had experienced in the past, and he knew he needed to look past the tone to focus on the words. Nya expertly began shaving Lavon.

The problem was now starting to take shape in Lavon's mind. Nya stopped shaving for the moment and stared at Lavon as though now was his only chance to respond.

"I told Webber I would be there if he wanted to talk. Frankly, the whole process they are discussing is a little hard for me to wrap my mind around. I come from middle Mississippi, and we have a process for getting a woman pregnant that has worked well for generations."

Nya put one hand on Lavon's forehead and moved it back, exposing his throat. "I must admit this is my favorite part of shaving a man." She began shaving Lavon's neck while he sat frozen, wondering if she accepted his last comments without reservation.

Nya covered Lavon's face with a warm towel. "I see us as friends. It would be hurtful if you conspired against me. I am not sure that what Shelia is proposing is a good idea, and I need time to think about it."

"No matter what you and Wendell decide, I will not push one way or the other."

"Good. Now that that is resolved, I need to trim the mop you are growing and calling hair."

WENDELL AND SAM TYLER were in one of the church rooms helping Lavon with his tuxedo. Lavon told Wendell of his frightening experience at Nya's hands and how the misunderstanding had concluded.

"Son, I think this is the best haircut and shave you have ever gotten. You look downright presentable. Now that being said, why would someone from this century even consider letting someone shave them with a piece of 1600 technology, were there no sharp rocks or broken glass available?" Sam asked.

"Dad, I think you miss the point." Lavon attempted to correct.

"Don't smart off to your father. That is rude." Wendell added.

"Thank you, son; these kids today seem to think you can say something rude and simply adjust the tone, and that makes it less rude, like when someone bumps into you and then yells excuse me in your face. And pardon me, I don't mean to sound like an old fuddy-duddy about things. I know your generation has everything well at hand, and old guys like me need only to pick the spot where we plan our final rest. But before you guys start throwing dirt on me, let me ask a couple of things." Sam Tyler began as she helped Wendell adjust Lavon's bow tie.

"Oh, Oh, here it comes. Words of wisdom." Lavon stated.

"I said, be nice to your father, and don't take for granted what I never had," Wendell added.

"Thank you, my son. As I was saying, Lavon, I would like for you to go out and cure cancer—not just some cancers but all cancers. It should not take a smart boy like you long; you can take the whole day if you need to. And Wendell, I would like for you to solve world hunger and bring about worldwide peace."

Lavon and Wendell both look confused.

"You boys look a little confused."

"All right, Dad, what are we missing?" Lavon had to ask.

"Well, it would appear to me that the one major task the men of my generation are entrusting to the men of your generation is assisting in the procreation of the species. Yet you have time on your hands to research ways to foul up the time-honored process. Good for you. Because from where I stand as the father of so many knuckleheads, the women of our species have signed up to do the really hard part. And have for centuries done so."

"Dad, I don't know if the issue is that simple." Lavon confided.

"What is not simple is that your brother Norbert has six children and another on the way, and he is busy working at his auto repair shop. But I have not heard of him and Alice mixing up a baby like a high school science project."

Wendell looked at Lavon, and Lavon returned the look. It was clear that they both were searching their thoughts for a logical counterargument to combat the raging tide of logic flowing from Sam Tyler.

"You see, lads, I have always been a practical man. I have, I think, raised my children to be as pragmatic as possible. If, at this time, you are searching your vast reservoir of knowledge for a suitable retort, don't bother. It is not me that will suffer the consequences of a poor choice in this case."

"You know they call them safety razors for a reason, and I have plenty at the house." Wendell informed Lavon. "My wife can be a little unsettled at times. I love her with all my heart, but I would never let her shave me with one of those things. What did you feel you had to prove, and who do you think you had to prove it to."

"Women can all be slightly unsettled at times; that's the fun part," Sam commented.

"She is upset about Shelia." Lavon attempted to correct.

"So again, my being old and all, I don't see the problem. If this Shelia, whoever she is, wants a baby, why doesn't she go to a bar, take some guy home, and put on some Jonny Mathis records, and presto."

"Records may make a comeback long before Jonny Mathis," Lavon informed.

"I get your point, sir, but Sheila is gay. She is married to Webber; you met her. She is one of my best friends." Wendell tried to close the understanding gap.

"The principle has remained the same for years. So why don't you and your good friend just do the horizontal bossa nova? If your friend is gay, it shouldn't mean a thing to her sexually." Sam reasoned. "And if you lay down as friends, you get up as friends."

"When I walked down the aisle with Nya, she now owns everything in my underwear, so she gets a say-so," Wendell explained.

"Fair enough, then that means Nya and Webber need to talk." Sam's comment was simple wisdom, but once again, he had cut to the root of an issue. "Besides, using a massive group of people to produce one child seems a little excessive to me. There, you are donating the juice, the lovely Webber is donating the egg, Shelia is carrying the baby, and a team of college graduates is facilitating the process. It would appear to me that you, young people, are so busy looking for an easier way to do things that you are mucking it all up."

"Do you think so?" Wendell was now listening intently.

"I think your wife has issues because it forever ties you to this Shelia person. Your wife, for all practical intents and purposes, has allowed you one emotional infidelity in your life, and now you ask for a second."

"I never thought about it that way."

"If I were the type of person that makes suggestions under such circumstances."

Lavon made a harsh sound of clearing his throat, but his father ignored the hint and continued. "I would propose that yes, you will do it only if Nya agrees, and it can be your friend Webber, whom you love and trust, who carries the baby. And I strongly recommend that you suggest that you and Webber do it the old-fashioned way. Anything gained too easily is disrespected or disregarded just as easily in the long run."

"So that's been settled. Why are you still tackling people?" Wendell asked Lavon.

"He started it," Lavon commented.

"On this day, it is customary for the father to give his son a sage piece of advice. My advice to you, my sons. Don't have fourteen children you would be surprised how many of them turn to be knuckleheads."

Wendell considered Lavon's answer, and his only response was. "Yes, Sir, I see your point."

LYNN HAD AWAKENED SEVERAL times during the night, reaching for Lavon. That's right, you told him to sleep elsewhere for this night out of superstition. The nightmares had come back, and Lavon had a way of guarding her through the night, protecting her from the kramerias that lured in her past. Somewhere during the morning, Rosa, her maid, had told her it was time to get ready, but she was unaware if she had responded. Joan Patterson, her friend and the wife of F.B.I. agent Tim Patterson, was helping her get dressed to go to the church.

"I love him so much. I know it was something a teenage girl might say, but I really do. Are you sure it's me that he wants to marry?" Lynn heard herself asking Rebecca Tyler, Lavon's mother. Somewhere, during the process of turning her into a bride, Rebecca Tyler and Joanne Dodd appeared. Rebecca Tyler and Joanne Dodd were as different as women could be. Still, they worked together as if they had total control over the situation. Joanne Dodd was organizer and consultant to her brother Dolan. Dolan was an underworld kingpin and known for his harsh methods. When Barbara, Joanne's sister, took off for the bright lights of Hollywood, Joanne found herself, with the assistance of Rosa, one of the maids, engaged in the duties of playing mom for a lonely Lynn. Joanne had often regretted not protesting Lynn's first marriage to Masterson, the enforcer, but Joanne's fear of losing the connection she had grown to value with Lynn outweighed her best intentions.

Joan Patterson was there to be the maid of honor and a resource for the shakiness that seemed to be the order of the day. Joan Patterson was a friend to Lynn. Joan is a doctor at the local hospital, and her husband is an F.B.I. agent, Tim Patterson. Joan had met Lavon and had enlisted his help in solving a problem that was crippling the hospital. Joan had quickly become a fan of Lavon and when he facilitated the rescue of Nya, a friend of hers Joan knew Lavon's true worth as an investigator.

"He loves you, Lynn. He wants to make it official in front of friends, family, and God." Rebecca responded as a hairdresser worked on Lynn's hair.

"And the baby. Will he love the baby?" Lynn murmured.

Joanne, Joan, and the hairdresser stared at Rebecca Tyler, clearly aware that Rebecca possessed information they did not.

"Lynn baby, my son loves children. He is going to love this more, especially."

Lavon was led down the aisle with his father, Sam Tyler, on one side and his best man, Wendell Bishop, on the other. Loud organ music played, and the pews were filled with people. There were T.V. cameras because Mayor Carlton Dodd, one of Lynn's uncles, was here for the wedding. Barbara Dodd took every opportunity to accost the camera operators, the reporters, and the new media to remind them how great she still is. None of this seemed to matter as Lavon walked forward; it was as if he were descending into a tidal pool of distorted reality. Lavon had played football in front of massive crowds in college. Lavon had chased criminals and been injured in the process. Lavon had served in military operations where survival was unsure. Still, nothing in the past had ever caused him this much disorientation.

"It aint too late to back out now. If you make a run for the door, I've got you covered." Lavon heard a woman's voice. It was Abby joking, standing next to his brother Bobby Joe.

"Handle that woman, Bobby Joe," Sam joked back, which caused everyone in hearing range to laugh.

The alter was getting closer, but Lavon could not remember when he had last signaled his legs to walk.

Nya walked over to Wendell and kissed her husband lightly on the cheek as he prepared to walk forward with Lavon. Lavon felt Nya put something in his outer tuxedo pocket, but his mind was not yet clear enough to wonder about what it was.

When Lavon reached the altar, he could see the minister's mouth moving but couldn't hear the words. Lavon followed the minister's eyes and turned around to see what was happening behind him.

THERE WAS A KNOCK AT the door. Joan opened the door, and Terrell's massive hulking frame stood there, consuming all view. 'I have a bunch of little ladies here that say they came for a wedding, and the only thing missing is a bride," Terrell stated boldly. Terrell was a black giant of a man who worked for the Sheriff's department. Terrell was known as the babysitter for the judges. Their security ultimately fell into his hands, and he took his responsibility seriously.

"This day would not be complete without you, old friend." Lynn bounded from her seat and gave Terrell a warm hug. Terrell returned the hug and stepped aside, revealing Anita, Jody, Noreen, Paden, and Sabrina. Anita was holding the bridal boutique. Anita passed to Lynn. "Alright, get your head in the game. It is time to turn on the lights of Broadway. Do you remember how to do that?"

"Roger that quarterback." Something in the confidence in the statement from Lynn and that shown in the faces of the Tyler girls was restoring her to the mature judge he had become. Lynn began to cast off the scared little girl part of her that had slowly invaded her thoughts fueled by her mother's visit. Lavon was waiting for her to step forth and be his wife somewhere. When Lynn had visited Lamont, Mississippi, she had heard snippets of stories of how Samuel Rowen Tyler, now the retired fiction writer, had, in his earlier days, tracked down and brought escaped criminals from three different continents. There was no doubt this man could walk his son down the aisle and secure him until the ceremony could begin.

THERE SHE WAS. LAVON could see her even though she wore a veil. It was his Lynn. No one else's Lynn but his. Mayor Carlton Dodd led the vailed Lynn halfway down the aisle, then handed her over to Dolan Dodd, another of Lynn's uncles. Lynn wore an off-white wedding dress with a long train. With Lynn now by his side, some of Lavon's focus was starting to restore itself. Lavon noticed the Sheriff's Department officers standing around the room in uniform. The Sheriff's department guards the judges, and it took a moment for Lavon to remember that Lynn was a judge.

"I LOVE YOU, MR. TYLER." Above the distortion of the day, Lavon could hear Lynn say this as clearly as anything he had ever heard in his life. And now his head was in the game.

Chapter Ten: The Wedding Toast and Couples Dance

Joanne Dodd had hired a wedding coordinator the assist Rebecca Dodd with setting up the wedding, since the wedding had special circumstances, like the mayor, local and international crime figures and the Sheriff's department all in one room. With the acceptance of the coordinators assistance Rebecca had made some hard and fast rules. One was that the wedding be a two-part ceremony. The first part be the exchanging of vows in Lynn's church in Shepherd's Pass. The exchange of vows ceremony had to come with a couple's dance. One of Tyler's beliefs was that a family wedding binds a man and woman and reaffirms the union of marriage. This concept is best celebrated by couples dancing harmoniously to reinforce the union that has been bestowed upon the new couple. By showing solidarity the united couples invite other couples and possible couples to seek a safe harbor in the union of marriage. At the end of the ceremony, there would be a couple dance. All available Tyler family members and their dance partners would join in a dance that was led by the new couple. At the end of the dance a circle would be formed and couple complete the dance would kiss. The kiss would be led by the groom's parents and proceed in the circle with the couple kissing until the married couple was finally reached, which would single accepted into the marriage union. The more couples that joined, the better in that it represented not only the joining of the married couple to the new family but also the unity between the husband and wife. When the tradition was created it was explained that couples often times my not agree or like the decision of their partner, but the circle of love and respect was there to guide them back to the love and trust of this day.

The second part of the wedding would be a reception, with the groom bringing his new wife to his church on the first Sunday and welcoming her not only into his church but also into the lives of his family and friends. This part would be done when Lavon and Lynn appeared in Shepherd's Pass.

AFTER EXCHANGING THE vows, everyone reassembled in the church reception area and prepared for the dance and toast to signal the couple's sendoff.

Lovester, Lavon's younger brother, and Paden Dodd performed two love duet love songs that a professional artist could not have performed better. Lovester had written the songs, and now he knew the vocal range of Paden, so not only did they both wow the listener, but they had fun singing them.

As per the traditional rules of wedding ceremony Lavon and Lynn danced together the first dance. It would have been crystal clear even to a casual observer that these two people were in love. It was not just their movements that were hormonally in step. Still, their very facial expressions showed a commingling of their lives was fully in process.

The next dance was the groom's father with the bride. Sam Tyler, being a retired police chief, novelist, and sometime advisor to the F.B.I., may have been an expert in many areas. Still, clearly, dancing was not one of Sam's areas of expertise. But it did not seem to matter. Lynn genuinely enjoyed the dance with her somewhat cantankerous new father-in-law.

It was now time for Lavon to dance with the mother of the bride. Lavon did a short, uncomfortable dance with Barbara. The camera flashed, and people moved around to get pictures of the faded star dancing with her new son-in-law. After this dance, Lavon requested that he dance with Joanne Dodd.

"Thank you," Lavon whispered to Joanne as they danced, and the thanks needed no explanation.

"At this time, as part of the groom's family tradition, we are preparing for the couple's dance. This dance will be led by those friends and family invited to be part of the couple's dance. Then, when instructed, any and all couples that wish to reaffirm the union of love and trust here today are invited to join," the coordinator announced.

The smooth sound of a county singer began in a heartfelt classic that called lovers to dance.

"Excuse me, Mister Tyler. Your sister Noreen has explained this part of your family tradition, and I would so much like to take part," Paden said to Lovester, then led him to the dance floor. Paden winked at Noreen as Noreen and Eric took their positions on the dance floor.

"Now that your brother is married, does that mean you are planning to return to Lamont?" Paden asked, hoping her fear that Lovester would say yes would not give her away.

"Well, I have been living in Lynn's house, and a man needs to stand on his own two feet." Lovester answered.

"Why can't those feet be here?"

"I don't know what there is for me here," Lovester responded, and the look in Paden's eyes told him he had said the exact wrong thing.

"You could stay here, and I would help you find a place to live. You could keep working at the Smokehouse." Paden attempted now to let Lovester know he had to voice his reservations.

"What about that English fellow that I heard is so hot and bothered for you?"

"Lovester, the guy is an actor. My family and some of its contacts fund movies. You have heard of girls that sleep their way to the top. Well, there are some guys that do it too."

"It aint right for a fellow to use a woman in such a way."

"Lovester, I am no angel, and I come from a hard side of my family, but I ask that you consider sticking around for a little while." Paden rested he head against Lovester's chest as they danced. Paden could hear the beating of Lovester's heart and she hoped the beating was for her.

"ERIC, I THINK YOU ARE a great guy, but I would be lying if I told you I have completely gotten over Simon, the guy that died in my arms trying to protect me from some maniac," Noreen stated as she could see telltale signs of Eric descending his thoughts of wondering about her.

"Anita has been with us for a short while, and she asked me to come and dance with you. A dance is my only expectation. I think I would be fortunate if you had me as a friend."

Noreen pulled Eric closer to her and rested in his simplicity. "Thank you, Eric, maybe we will be friends, but keep in mind I am not as fragile as I look."

"HOW ARE THE RIBS HOLDING up?" Jody asked Wade. Wade Vaughn, her dance partner, was her partner in the Mississippi Bureau of Investigation. Wade had recently been shot and was not yet cleared to return to duty. The doctors had voiced some reservations about his drive to Missouri from Mississippi. The bullet scrapped and fractured his rib. The person shooting Wade made the novice mistake of getting excited when he fired and shot at the gun; not the center of Wade, or Wade would be dead. The shooter would not have the opportunity to learn from his mistake in that he was now dead.

"I think they hurt but to tell the truth dancing with you is quite the distraction."

"Keep talking like that, and I am all yours, Detective Wade Vaughn."

"SO, WHAT MADE YOU AGREE to come this far for a dance, Mr. Tyler?" Anita asked her dance partner, Andrew Tyler.

"There was something in meeting you—a total fluke. Random chance, but there it was. Something about the encounter made me want to know you more."

"Strange, I had the same feeling."

"I apologize for my overly nosey sister asking your brother questions about your intentions. My sister works as my mother's assistant campaign manager, and my sister somehow feels I will run for office one day."

"And she doesn't want any skeletons rattling out of your closet."

"Nicely stated. Maybe too nicely."

"I understand how family can be concerned about you, and maybe how they express it goes a little off the rails."

"Someone told me you are a quarterback?"

"So why should boys have all the fun?"

IT WAS NOW BOBBY JOE'S turn to lead Abby onto the dance floor. Abby could detect a certain pride in Bobby Joe's step as he walked with her. "I really am not a good dancer, but anything for the cause." Abby joked.

"Do you love him?" Bobby asked Abby as he noticed Abby glance at Lavon and Lynn dancing.

"I think it is more complicated than that. Being a simple girl, I struggle to wrap my head around it. This whole covenant of the blood thing your father talked about. Maybe there is a lot of truth to that."

"He loves you." Abby was amazed at Bobby Joe's comment.

"He has Lynn."

"And in many relevant ways, he has you too. Don't worry, I am not jealous. I just want you to be truthful to yourself."

"So, if we are exposing each other's souls, tell me what happened to the girl they say you were dating?"

"My little sister has a big mouth." Bobby smirked and danced. "She was seeing someone else, and I knew it. I suppose he knew about me too. One day, I told her she had to make a choice."

"And she chose him over you."

"I learned a valuable lesson that day. Ultimations hurt."

"Bullshit. Bullshit, Robert Joseph Tyler, the truth is all you; Tyler boys are tough as nails on the outside. Look at your brother, Lester. He jumps in front of a girl he hardly knew at the time and takes a bullet. Lavon beat a guy half to death for disrespecting me before he had any idea if I was salvageable."

"What's your point?"

"The point is the harder you Tyler boys are on the outside, the softer you are on the inside. Not all females are like your mom. You are not guaranteed to find some nearsighted girl with bad skin and an overbite so you can take her home and have a couple of dozen kids."

"I am not sure, but did you just insult my mother?"

"No. I love your mom and we have not yet even met. The point I am trying to make is that there are girls out here in the world who make a point of abusing smart, sensitive guys. The only possible reason the girl that left you for the other guy left is because she knew with him, she was free to fool around. And that is probably why your sisters have taken an oath to protect you, poor bastards. I would be willing to bet everything I have that this girl that walked away from you is going to show her sorry ass up the first chance she gets to play; come rescue me, or no one understands me the way you do."

"Abby."

"What?"

"I think I like you." Boddy Joe confessed.

"Good."

"And there are two things I need to tell you."

"Go for it." Abby prompted.

"First, my brother's name is Lovester."

"I thought that was what I said."

"Second, the tradition for this dance ends with a kiss. It is the welcoming of the new couple to the fold. This is a circle best left unbroken."

"So, if you were dancing with your sister, would it symbolize a break in the link?" Abby surmised.

"Exactly."

"So, you are giving me advanced notice this time before you kiss me."

"Thought it only fair." Bobby chuckled.

"Bring it on tough guy."

"SAM, I WON'T RUIN MY son's wedding with a temper tantrum, but why did you give Clarkson and his F.B.I. spies Anita?"

"A matter of top-secret national security, sweetheart." Sam Tyler was prepared to make his lumps.

"Sam, I think I can understand someone having an affair with someone they work with. A one-time thing, you know, helping a friend gets a little out of control. But Clarkson held both women as his wife for some time."

"I am told he has mellowed with age."

"They say the same thing about you, but here you are, crusty as ever." Rebecca laughed.

They continued to dance the dance of two people that had for a lifetime and a half and seen each other through the ebb and flow of life.

The couple had journeyed through sickness and the struggle of raising a large family together.

" So, Sam here is my position. I don't want to see any of my kids as an anonymous star of some government wall. Not just because I love them. But also, because I know how much you love them, despite you best efforts to prove otherwise. I know what it would do to you, and I know there is just enough of the old Samual Rowen Tyler in you, that is someone hurt anyone of them you would go after them and heaven help their souls. Promise me one thing: if any of our children want to come home and stop saving the world at any point, you will not fault them."

"You have my promise."

And as the senior Tyler couple danced a timeless love permeated the room.

"AND NOW, IF ALL THOSE wishing to celebrate the union that God has set before us wish to join in, you may now join the couple's dance," the wedding coordinator announced—the dance floor filled with guests dancing and enjoying the tradition. The couples kissed and applauded the blessing of the union of husband and wife.

After the dance, it was time for the toast to send the couple off into their new life. Sam Tyler stood in the center of the floor, raising a glass of champagne, and was preparing to make a toast. Lynn and Lavon stood beside Sam Tyler. Rebecca Tyler walked up and removed the champagne from Lynn's hand and handed her a goblet of water instead. Lynn reached over, took a fork from a nearby table, and started tapping the water glass.

"Before my new father-in-law makes his toast, I want to make an announcement." Lynn started and waited until she had everyone's attention. "My new husband plans to take to an Island in Hawaii that literally translated is the baby maker island, for our honeymoon." This brought a round of cheers from the gathers. "Exhibit A." Lynn pointed to Nya. Nya stood up and sported the pregnant belly. "My dear Lavon does not know that he has already done the deed as they say."

Lavon grabbed Lynn and kissed her. At that moment, seeing Nya, Lavon remembered Nya had put something in his pocket. Lavon removed the item; it was a pacifier. Lavon thought about Nya requesting that Lavon stay close to Lynn for the next few months. Lavon looked at Nya, and she winked.

"Damn these kids if they don't know how to upstage an old man." Sam Tyler joked.

ABBY STOOD WATCHING the chauffeur-driven limo with Just Married on the back drive Lavon and Lynn off. Abby was instinctually aware that she was in a crowd of people, but she felt totally alone for the first time in a long time. Bobby Joe stepped away to retrieve a call from his fire department unit.

Paden Dodd had caught the bridal bouquet with great effort, while Abby had made no effort to catch the symbolic flowers.

"You know, sometimes when you stand in one spot, you see something, and from that vantage point, it looks like the worst thing that could ever happen in your life." A woman's voice softly came from behind Abby. Abby was afraid to turn around. At one time, Abby may have been known for flippant smart-ass comments and a quick wit, but now Abby was afraid whatever look she had on her face might betray what was really going on in her head.

"Of course, often at those times, if you step six inches to the left or six inches to the right, you may see that what you are seeing is the best thing that could ever possibly be happening." Rebecca Tyler continued. "I am concerned that despite my best efforts to fatten you up, you are still so skinny."

Compelled by a force deep within herself, Abby turned around and warmly hugged Rebecca Tyler.

"You know you and Lynn have something in common," Rebecca whispered.

Abby wanted to pull away from the hug, but there was something almost therapeutic about it, and she could not.

"Neither of you girls had your natural mother available at a time when that is the most important in a young girl's life. I can tell." Rebecca stated. "But that alright cause I am here now, Abigail. And if you were wondering if the tea you have been drinking all evening is going to be strong enough to help you make it through the night. Or if the puppy of yours I have heard about would be able to handle a sudden change in its puppy parent. Don't worry. You are stronger than even you think. And if you need help, I will stand shoulder to shoulder with you and help keep the demons at bay."

Abby missed the opportunity to respond or comment.

"There you two are. Momma, I see you met Abby. Don't you think she is as beautiful as Lovester was telling everyone?" Bobby Joe had returned.

"I need to hire that kid as a public relations person," Abby commented.

"Yes, she is," Rebecca commented. "Abby and I have been corresponding."

"Your mother and your sister Kim are my sugar suppliers. How did your call go?" Abby was in a hurry to switch the focus of the conversation to anything other than herself.

"I have to leave. There is a truck that was found in a creek near a bridge. The truck is registered to Shavon Crabtree; state police say she is a person of interest in a couple of shootings. The local cops want my guys to search the waters."

"Shavon," Abby commented. "A.K.A. Calamity Jane."

"Do you know her?" Bobby Joe asked.

"Unfortunately, I do, and they are probably wasting your time searching the waters. Or at least for her. She seems to walk away from even the greatest disasters. But of course, the anyone standing near her is never that lucky."

"Probably, but some of my guys don't get along well with the state cops, so I have to referee. But I want a second date to show what a nice guy I am. And my mom is my witness if you agree."

Abby smiled as she noticed Bobby Joe standing six inches to her right, and Rebecca was smiling. "Yes, Bobby, I will happily go out with you."

Also by Alex Mitchell

Welcome to Shepherds Pass
Revenge at Shepherds Pass
Treasure at Shepherds Pass
Welcome to Shepherds Pass
Man Among the Missing
Noreen Tyler
Robinhood at Shepherds Pass
That Which Makes Us Who We Are
Secrets That Bind Family
Balance of Power in Shepherds Pass
All Gods Children
The Mole Hunters Children
Anita Tyler and the Puzzles of Mass Destruction
The Wedding at Shepherds Pass